Jackson's hospital bed started up a ramp that led to something like an assembly line.

Mechanical arms were mounted at intervals, tipped with glittering implements. Fierce white lights beamed down.

He glanced anxiously ahead. His bed was approaching the first of the machines, a fearsome thing with multiple arms terminating in stethoscope, tongue depressor, rubber mallet, blood-pressure collar, hypodermic needle and some other gadgets that looked like a big pair of pliers and a saber saw.

With desperate strength, Jackson managed to chop off the restraining straps around his shoulders with his artificial hand. He rolled over and fell painfully onto the concrete floor. The bed trundled on without him, under the machine's scanners, which searched up and down in puzzlement while a big metal finger prodded the empty sheets . . .

"LESS THAN HUMAN is funny, fast-paced, an enjoyable read. Those without a sense of humor can skip it in favor of some square-jawed space epic—at their loss."
—Gregory Benford, author of
TIMESCAPE and ARTIFACT

"LESS THAN HUMAN is that rarity among novels—a genuinely funny book. I was both amused and amazed."
—Edward Bryant

Other top-flight science fiction
from Avon Books

THE CHROMOSOMAL CODE
by Lawrence Watt-Evans

EARTHMAN'S BURDEN
by Poul Anderson and Gordon R. Dickson

SARABAND OF LOST TIME
by Richard Grant

THE TIMESERVERS
by Russell M. Griffin

Less Than Human

ROBERT CLARKE

AVON
PUBLISHERS OF BARD, CAMELOT, DISCUS AND FLARE BOOKS

For Gwyneth Cravens

With thanks to Edward Bryant, John Clute, and
Jodie Manasevit

AVON BOOKS
A division of
The Hearst Corporation
1790 Broadway
New York, New York 10019

Copyright © 1986 by Charles Platt
Published by arrangement with the author
Library of Congress Catalog Card Number: 85-91195
ISBN: 0-380-89992-2

First Avon Printing, April 1986

AVON TRADEMARK REG. U. S. PAT. OFF. AND IN
OTHER COUNTRIES, MARCA REGISTRADA, HECHO EN
U.S.A.

Printed in the U.S.A.

K–R   10   9   8   7   6   5   4   3   2   1

Contents

Cast of Characters
In Order of Appearance

Eddie   Lunar missile systems technician and Mainframe Class Genocide player, he doubles as Keeper of the Big Steel Tank.

Crosby   Surfer (retired) and flowerperson, relocated in Chrysler Building Commune, waging a lonely battle against sexual deprivation and senility.

Melanie   Sweet, sixteen, and lonely, she rejects the degenerates of the commune that nurtured her, and pledges herself to purity, decency, romance, and rock and roll.

Lennon   Guru of the Chrysler Building, father of Melanie, warden of the freaks.

Henry Jackson   New York City Police Chief working obsessively to inflict cruel and unusual punishment on ethnic minorities and other deviant enemies of the status quo.

Cynthia Jackson   Wife of the above, her only distraction from terminal hypochondria is total-immersion TV.

Chief Programmer   Onetime token black at IBM, now global dictator. Disenchanted with humanity, he prefers automatons for those intimate moments of relaxation.

Sullivan   Onetime President of the United States, exiled in obscurity while his prosthetic look-alike occupies the Oval Office.

Charlotte   Beautiful blonde with a bionic brain: the Chief Programmer's mistress, confidante, and sex toy.

Mick   Forty-year-old hoodlum gadget freak who brews bootleg oxygen amid mounds of memorabilia.

Sanchez   Veteran police sergeant, used to reside in Harlem before it was demolished and replaced with bombproof underground luxury apartments.

B.E.R.T.H.A. (aka Burt)   Amnesiac, indistinguishable from a human being, he was grown in a tank as humanity's savior or nemesis, depending on one's point of view.

Mistress Ursula   Taoist grandmother, numerologist, and homeopath, she casts the I-Ching and counsels commune members against techno-fetishism.

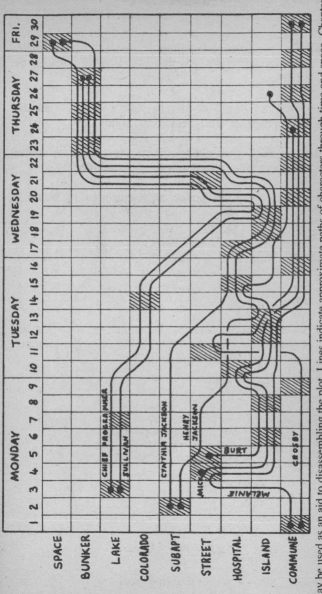

May be used as an aid to disassembling the plot. Lines indicate approximate paths of characters through time and space. Chapters are indicated as shaded rectangles. Characters who do not change location (e.g., Lennon) have been omitted for clarity.

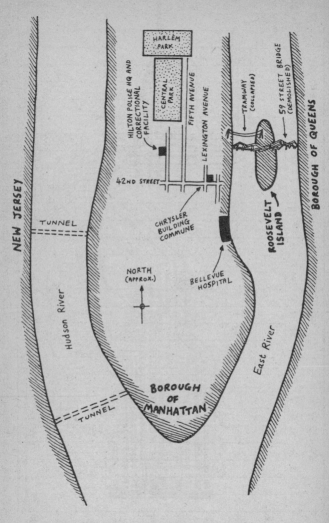

NEW YORK CITY IN THE YEAR 2010

(not drawn to scale)

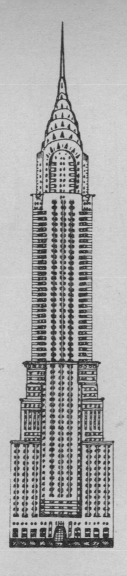

THE CHRYSLER BUILDING

(viewed from Lexington Avenue)

PROLOGUE

Living on the Moon was boring; that was the trouble. Eddie jabbed the big red button with his elbow, and the air lock opened with a groaning, gasping noise—the same kind of noise Eddie had been making himself just lately, when he woke up each morning and remembered where he was. He checked his suit leakage indicator, shouldered his big black plastic bag, and stepped out into the lunar landscape.

The blotchy cream-and-purple disk of Planet Earth hung in the black velvet sky. Eddie gave it a baleful glance, thinking about all the people down there—or up there, whichever it was—mowing their lawns, buying groceries, going out on dates, maybe some of them looking at the Moon right now. Little did they realize they were looking at him, Eddie, in Mare Imbrium, taking out the garbage.

He kicked a lumpy lunar rock out of his way. Here he was on his patriotic tour of duty, guarding the farthest outpost of the Free World's nuclear deterrent, and what happened? Nothing happened, that's what happened.

He trudged to the edge of a small cliff, his breathing sounding loud inside the suit helmet. He tossed the garbage bag over the edge and watched it land on top of a huge heap of similar bags, making them stir and tumble in slow motion under the low gravity.

Eddie started back to the installation. Over in the distance, at the foot of some spiky mountains, a space probe from some bygone decade lay like a smashed light bulb in the primordial dust. Eddie ignored it. He followed his own footprints to the air lock, shut the hatch behind him, shed his suit, and wearily went through entry verification. Voice-print, fingerprint, palmprint—security was tight up here, they weren't going to let just anyone wander in. Only him, Eddie, overseeing the automatic systems, eating frozen dinners, playing computer games, watching TV, and wiping dust off the panic buttons while the death machines slumbered in their silos.

Well, it could have been worse, Eddie told himself as he reentered narrow corridors hewn from lunar rock. The place was bombproof, and there was enough recycled air, food, and water to sustain life almost indefinitely—which was more than most people could currently expect on Planet Earth. Even millionaires had power outages and water-contamination problems these days, down in their underground penthouses. Once in a while you'd see an item on the news: an air-feed pipe would rust through or get clogged with mud, and Mr. and Mrs. Megabucks would be flopping around gasping like beached fish, their desiccated flesh discovered months later by maintenance robots. The U.S. Space Forces took better care of you than that, for sure.

He made his way into the control room, a snug cubicle that flickered in the light from dozens of malfunctioning video screens. Half the systems in the base were currently defective, one way or another, including the computer that was supposed to run everything. Eddie knew he ought to try to do something about it, but the library of video games in his living module was a constant distraction. A half-finished game of Genocide was waiting for him right now, as soon as he finished his daily inspection tour.

He ran his finger down the checklist. One more task remained, as he well knew: check Bertha. Well, that shouldn't take more than a minute. He squeezed down another passageway to a part of the installation that contained a special research project. Inside a small circular chamber was a huge stainless steel tank on which had been glued an imitation brass plaque:

Biosynthesis of Extraneous Radio Transmission
via Holographic Accretion
U.S. Space Forces Private Property
R. Folsom Sullivan
President of the United States of America

Bertha, for short. Some kind of robot was being built in there, and it was "too secret" to be done on Earth. That was all Eddie knew. Sometimes, when he couldn't sleep, he came and peered in the window of the tank like a restless customer at a laundromat. Inside was a lumpy mess like an automobile seat losing its padding, suspended in what looked like raspberry Jell-O, shot through with radiant white beams that danced around like knitting needles. The whole thing made an irritating droning noise.

But when Eddie peered in now, the little white lights weren't moving, the droning noise had stopped, and a big red light was flashing. "Just what I needed," he muttered.

"Please repeat, Eddie," said a voice from a grille in the ceiling.

"You screwed up," Eddie shouted. "You got offline. How come the alarm didn't trip?"

"The alarm is malfunctioning, Eddie. I informed you last week."

"Well, all right, but you still could have said something." He sighed and went to an instruction manual chained to a steel shelf against the wall. He flipped through thick celluloid pages covered in pictograms. "Press the green button," he muttered to himself, "hold it down till you hear a beep, pull the yellow lever, then file a report on the red form with the yellow edges." He went over the procedure a couple more times till he was sure he'd got it straight. These tasks existed because peace activists on Earth insisted on having a human being wired into the strategic defense system. So here he was, wired in. He hoped it gave everyone back home a real sense of security.

He went and pressed the green button, waited for a beep, pulled the yellow lever, then checked the tank again. The white beams of light jerked and resumed moving. The droning noise started up.

"What happened?" Eddie asked as he made his way back to his cubicle. "Was there a break in transmission?" As he understood it, a station in Texas was beaming data up to the Moon, where it was received and fed into the tank where the robot was being built. That was how they were programming the robot, using instructions sent from Earth.

"A solar flare interrupted data acquisition," the installation's computer told him. "You must file a report on the red form with the yellow edges."

Eddie sat down and considered his options. If he filed the form, it would look as if he'd screwed up somehow, even though it wasn't his fault the alarm hadn't gone off. On the other hand, if he didn't file the form, no one would know anything about it—that is, until the robot finally stepped out of its tank and was short of a few minutes of data. It wouldn't know something it ought to; wouldn't be able to name the capital of Kentucky or some dumb thing.

Hell, it probably wouldn't matter. Eddie picked up a sheet of plain white paper and fed it into the document slot. "There you go."

"Thank you, Eddie."

The whole system was stupid. He turned back to the infinitely more interesting game of Genocide he'd been playing. To win, you had to wipe out the other half of the world before you got wiped out yourself. After three months on the Moon, Eddie was already a Mainframe Class player. He typed instructions on the console, to withdraw five billion Swiss francs from his plutonium bullion reserves and stage an accident in South African bacteriological labs conveniently located near a training field for airplane hijackers financed by Moslem fanatics. That should get things going at the U.N. He watched with obsessive interest as symbols danced across the video screen, and soon forgot his claustrophobic surroundings, the idiot computer, the real world in general, and the passing of time itself.

Meanwhile, inside the stainless steel tank, Bertha the ultra-secret experimental robot had resumed building protein chains, accreting neurons, growing fingernails, and learning to do addition sums. But the break in transmission had made more of a difference than Eddie realized. When Bertha finally stepped out into the world, that difference would show.

I. EMERGENCY EXIT

"Crosby?" The voice was shy and sweet and very feminine, calling softly from outside the bead curtain that hung across the doorway.

Crosby blinked. "Huh?"

"It's me, Melanie. You said yesterday that I should stop by."

"Oh. Yeah." He rubbed his eyes, crawled from his mattress of decaying foam rubber to his pile of dirty laundry, found an old caftan that wasn't too wrinkled, and pulled it over his pallid sixty-five-year-old flesh. He glanced around at the squalor of his cubicle, realizing reluctantly that if he was to have any chance at all with this chick, he'd have to do something about the mess. "Gimme a minute," he called. He straightened his heaps of yellowing head comix, lit a stick of incense in lieu of an air freshener, and used an old astrology magazine to sweep dead matches and blanket fluff under the rush matting in the center of the bare concrete floor. Then he slumped back onto the mattress and started rolling a large joint. "Come on in."

The beads over the doorway were tentatively pushed aside by a slim, alabaster hand whose nails were painted Cutex Cute Tomata. "Hi," said Melanie.

"Make yourself comfortable." He gestured vaguely.

The mattress was the only thing to sit on. Melanie perched on the extreme end of it and primly rearranged the starched ruffles of her cancan slip. "What's up, Crosby?"

He lit his joint, inhaled deeply, and offered it to her. Melanie pretended not to notice. She linked her hands around her knees and studied the tops of her penny loafers.

Crosby let the smoke out of his scarred lungs. He took a deep breath and was seized by a sudden coughing fit, making his wizened old body twist and jerk. He groaned, crawled to the air purifier beneath the window, pressed his face to the vent, and upped the oxygen feed.

Melanie watched with grudging compassion. Despite her natural distaste for physical deterioration and poor personal hygiene, she hated to see any living thing suffer. "Are you okay?"

"No sweat." The fit subsided, and Crosby settled back onto the mattress, straightening his hairpiece absently. The vent had left pink-and-white indentations across his ravaged face.

"You should rest a minute," she told him.

"I'm hip." He took another toke and nodded his head in time to the Grateful Dead playing over the rewired Muzak system of the old office building. "Can you dig it?" he asked vaguely.

Melanie shook her head, making her ponytail bob. At sixteen, she was one of the youngest members of New York's Chrysler Building Commune (est. 1993). Most of them, like Crosby, were in their sixties, grooving together on the drug and music trips they'd shared decades ago in San Francisco, before it slid into the sea. Melanie had never been able to relate to their world; she painted her cubicle cherry blossom pink and charcoal gray and passed long, lonely days reading old *True Romance* magazines, pushing her cuticles back, and listening to vintage 45s of Bobby Vinton and the Everly Brothers.

"Just what did you want to talk about, Crosby?"

"Oh, you know." He fumbled for a roach clip, inhaled the last of his joint, and started rolling another. "Just wanted to hang out with you, rap a little. I mean, you're a groovy chick.'' He eyed Melanie's legs as she rerolled her bobby sox. "Sure you don't want a hit?" He offered her the second joint.

"No, thank you."

"You can't go on like this, Melanie. You gotta get turned on." He gestured vaguely toward a homemade psychedelic portrait of Timothy Leary pinned to the wall above a chipped plaster Buddha. "Gotta get into it, know what I mean?"

She gave him a vexed look. "We've discussed this before."

Crosby edged along the bed toward her. Simple lust flickered in his tired old bloodshot eyes. "C'mon, baby." He put his arm clumsily around her shoulders. "Let's fuck."

She shook his arm away. "Don't talk to me like that!"

"Hey, don't be so uptight."

She jumped to her feet. "Crosby, how many times do I have to explain, I do *not* want to go *all the way* with you." She turned away. "Thank God I taught myself to read, so I learned there are other ways than this to live." She stood and stared out of the window at shadowy shapes of nearby skyscrapers, barely visible in the morning smog. "Somewhere out there, there must be someone who feels the same way I do. Someone who still cares about fidelity, and love." She turned and glared at Crosby. "And cleanliness!"

He watched her wearily. "Melanie, you're living in the past. Gotta forget that plastic shit. Come back over here, just a little toke. Change your whole attitude."

"No! I will never allow myself to sink into this . . . this cesspool of depravity!"

Crosby winced. "Heavy." He shook his head and took a long, slow breath. "All right, if that's how it is. I been talking to your old man. Way he sees it, you're either on the bus or off the bus, you know?"

Melanie frowned. "What are you trying to tell me?"

"He said, if I can't get it on with you, if you won't, you

know, tune in, it's all over. Your vibes are so heavy, you're so uncool, you been bringing everyone down.''

Melanie shook her head in disbelief. ''Lennon said that? My own father?''

''Better believe it. You don't like it here, maybe you should move on out, get on the road, know what I mean?''

''Oh!'' Melanie turned quickly and ran out of the room.

Jefferson Airplane replaced the Grateful Dead. Crosby sighed, relit his second joint, and lay staring with hooded eyes at tattered Day-Glo posters of Middle Earth stapled to the ceiling. He turned on the black light.

''Too fucking much,'' he mumbled.

Melanie lowered the needle of her portable phonograph with a shaking hand. The sound of the Shangri-Las singing ''Never Go Home Anymore'' suddenly filled her cubicle. She sniffed back tears and resumed packing her baby blue travel case.

All along, she had clung to the faint hope that somehow she could convince her father to accept her the way she was. He was supposed to be so wise and understanding; he was the guru of the commune. And yet—

The door of her cubicle was thrown open and Lennon stood there—tall, wide, half-submerged in flowing white hair and beard. The plump skin peeking out of his satin sari was tattooed with butterflies, zodiac symbols, Tibetan mandalas, and alchemical formulae. He stood and glared at her. ''Peace,'' he said grimly, raising two fingers.

She stared at him resentfully. ''I'm running away from home.''

Lennon scratched his stomach. ''Well, I can relate to that.''

She slammed the lid of her suitcase. ''I never dreamed you could be so cruel.''

Lennon linked his hands across his stomach and studied his toes meditatively. ''Om,'' he said. ''Om, om, om. . . .''

Melanie increased the volume of the phonograph to maximum.

Lennon gave up. ''You don't understand how much

karma it's cost me, having a daughter like you," he shouted above the noise.

"Good. I'm glad."

"It's too bad your mother's not around. She would've known what to do." Melanie's mother had been an executive secretary in the days when businesses still rented space in the Chrysler Building. She had stayed on when the commune moved in, become one of Lennon's old ladies, and had even borne his child. But a year or so later she went out to buy some deodorant soap and never came back.

"My mother," Melanie said with a sob, "would tell me I'm a fool to stay in this horrible place where no one understands or cares about me."

Lennon shrugged. "So split."

"I will! I'm going!" She yanked the power cord out of its socket, and the music slowly ran down and died.

"You realize it's a jungle out there," he told her. "They don't give a shit about make-love-not-war."

"That's just fine." She picked up her suitcase in one hand, her phonograph in the other, and pushed past him.

"Don't come back till you've had a good fuck!" he shouted after her.

Her only response was another sob as she ran to the stairwell (the elevators hadn't worked since electricity was shut off in 1998) and hurried down the fifty flights to street level. "I hate him," she told herself unconvincingly, feeling the first qualms about her rash act as she forced open the emergency exit and stepped onto the eroded sidewalks of New York City, AD 2010.

2. INDISTINGUISHABLE FROM A HUMAN BEING

Meanwhile, two miles north and half a mile underground, Chief of Police Henry Jackson was dreaming. "Unlock this door or I'll break it down!" he bellowed in his dream, his rich baritone echoing through the tenement. He took his .45 from inside his jacket. His grip was firm and his hand steady. "I'm going to count to three!"

A cry of dismay came from within the apartment, and he heard a window being opened. He leveled the gun and shot the lock to pieces, then kicked the door in.

"Stay where you are, you!" he shouted at the young woman who stared back white-faced, one shapely leg over the window ledge. "I'd hate to have to kill a dame with such a pretty face."

Jackson's eyes narrowed with prurient interest as the woman put up her hands and walked meekly toward him. "Officer," she quavered, her young body showing plainly through a skimpy nightgown, "I'm sure you and I can come to some kind of agreement."

Jackson chuckled. "Well now, sweetheart, maybe we should go in the bedroom and talk this over." He gestured with his gun.

There was a sudden impact at the base of his spine. He jerked in surprise and his dream wavered. What—what was this? Someone behind him? He tried to hold onto his vision of the woman, but she faded and dissolved as the dream fell away and he opened his eyes to reality.

His wife was behind him, in bed with him in their

subapt, sheets wrinkled, air tasting stale, paint peeling off the ceiling six feet above. Carefully, Jackson turned his head, not making a sound.

His elephantine spouse lay with her eyes closed. Her knee was drawn up where it had struck him in his back. She was breathing quietly, regularly. Jackson wondered, Could she be faking? It was almost as if she had known what he'd been dreaming. Just how much *did* she know? He could never be certain, never be certain of anything.

He stifled a groan as he eased himself off the slab of sleeping foam and stood up. His joints clicked and creaked. His flesh was the same yellowing white as the walls of the subterranean apartment. He was thin, his hair was falling out, his eyes were bloodshot, his teeth were loose, he suffered horribly from hemorrhoids. He was sixty-two but looked closer to seventy-five.

His gnarled hands formed fists as he glared at his wife, still seemingly deep in slumber. He could never prove anything, that was the trouble. It was all circumstantial.

He bared his rotten teeth at her, then shuffled into the bathroom, automatically stooping to avoid the low ceilings. He used his two-quart freshwater ration to wash his face and shave, then padded into the kitchen cubicle and dialed some coffee. He sampled it and grimaced: it tasted acrid. It could be just the mixer fouling up again, or . . . there was only one way to find out.

He crept into the bedroom. His wife lay on the soiled sheets like a beached whale. Her face was masked by plastic skin restorer. A pink flannel nightdress covered her from her neck to her knees. *It's unfair*, Jackson thought. *Everything's unfair*.

He set the paper coffee cup down and shook her shoulder. "Morning, dearest."

She opened her eyes quickly. Maybe a little too quickly, he thought.

"I've brought you some coffee," he said.

She groaned and turned over. The bed sank under her as she moved. Jackson watched intently as she sipped the coffee. She winced and glared at him. "Henry, that beverage blender's been feeding us crap for *weeks*. Aren't you *ever* going to get them to fix it? Do I have to do *everything* around here myself?''

"So you're not going to drink it," he said.

"It stinks." She slumped down, one hand on her forehead.

"Something wrong, Cynthia?"

"Just leave me alone. I have a migraine."

Jackson eyed her dubiously and compressed his lips into a thin line. He gathered his clothes from the closet, pulled them over his withered flesh, and shuffled out into the adjoining cubicle that served as his office. He sank into his chair and sucked bacon-and-egg paste through the food tube, mixing in some synthetic Scotch and an antidepressant. It tasted wrong, like the coffee. Everything was screwed up. Not that it mattered: the civilized world was on the point of collapse, everyone knew that.

Many levels above, the city was in a state of terminal disintegration. Robot cops, programmed to shoot to kill when they witnessed any offense more serious than littering, kept the business district under control. Elsewhere, vigilante gangs attempted to impose some sort of law and order among the peps—peasant people, Third World immigrants who had turned the city into a vast refugee camp outside of the midtown Safe Zone.

Jackson yawned, glanced at the Monday-morning news sheet that had been disgorged by the telefax during the night, and discarded it. An image from his dream resurfaced in his weary brain. The girl had looked a lot like one of the women in his porn tapes—the pretty little Communist spy tied hand and foot for purposes of interrogation. He glanced guiltily at his watch, then selected the cassette from his secret collection. He reached for the viewing mask.

The picturefone chimed. Its screen lit up, showing a man's face. Breen!

Jackson pushed the cassette across the desk, out of sight. He ran a shaking hand through what was left of his hair and attempted to straighten his collar and sit up in his chair. He fumbled and pressed the accept button. "Yes sir, Commissioner!"

Breen eyed Jackson skeptically. "We seem to have a job for you, Jackson."

"Yes, sir. Of course, I'm somewhat overextended currently, working on the—"

"This has got a triple-A classification on it," Breen interrupted.

Triple-A? Jackson couldn't recall such a classification. It sounded bad. There were jackals in the department just waiting for him to make a blunder on a big case. That was why he always delegated the big cases. Apprehension spread through his guts.

"It's an escort job," Breen was saying. "Kind of unusual. The Pentagon has some kind of robot. It's less than human, you understand, but it eats, breathes, lives, and dies just like a real person. From the outside, it's indistinguishable from a human being."

Jackson blinked. "I didn't know they could do that."

"Good. You weren't meant to know." Breen gave him a thin smile. "Now, the snag is, this robot—it's their only prototype—has some kind of brain damage. Don't ask me why, but the psych people think they can figure out what's wrong with it by turning it loose and watching its reactions. Behavioral analysis. So, twenty of your best men are to escort this gadget wherever it wants to go."

"You mean *here*, sir? In New York?"

"Correct."

"But why not out in some desert somewhere? I mean, it's dangerous in New York City."

Breen sighed. "I know, I questioned it myself. But it seems this robot decided it wanted to wander around New York, and the scientists, ah, went along with its decision. You understand, this is kind of an important project; the robot's worth a trillion dollars; you'll be responsible."

Jackson gaped. He saw everything in sudden clarity. Someone, somewhere, had arranged this with the specific intention of ruining him. He thought he'd covered himself—employing yes-men, tapping their phones, having them followed, having the people who did the following followed. "Sir, I have a heavy work load and I think it would be more organizationally appropriate if the field department—"

"I'm sorry, Jackson." Breen sounded almost sympathetic. "But this directive has come straight down from the President."

Jackson paused. "You mean the White House President?"

"That's the one. It specifically states that the Chief of Police is to be responsible. And there's one other thing. The directive states that you must accompany your men with the robot at all times. Outside, for instance."

Jackson blinked. "Outside where?"

Breen shrugged. "Outside in the streets, wherever it wants to go."

"In the *streets?*" His voice was shrill.

"I know, it's irregular for a man of your rank. But that's what it says. Now, here's the physical description of the robot." He held up a sheet. "I'll put it through the telefax. The only important distinguishing feature is that the creature lacks a navel."

Was this really happening? Jackson touched his face to make sure he wasn't wearing the porn-tape viewing mask. Then he leaned closer to the screen and inspected Breen's image. Close up, all he could see were lots of little fizzing colored dots. You could never be sure, never be certain of anything.

"Jackson, is anything wrong?"

He straightened up quickly. "No sir."

"Hm. Well, a pedmobile will be waiting outside your subapt in fifteen minutes, to bring you in. You'll be heading the Bertha escort detail. That's the robot's name; it's an abbreviation. Bio-something of trans–something else. The technicians coined it, and it stuck. Stupid kind of a name, but the robot thinks of itself as Bertha, so we have to, even though I understand that its sex is male." Breen laughed as if he had made a small joke.

Jackson contrived the sick semblance of a grin. "Anything else, sir?"

"No, that's all. Good luck, Jackson. You'll need it on this one."

Jackson slumped in his chair as the screen went dark. He groaned and closed his eyes. A hopeful image of a tender young girl tied to a chair in a prison cell swam into his mind. She was naked, uncooperative, but helpless. The rubber truncheon was in his hand. . . .

No, no, that wasn't going to help. He staggered out of his office. "Cynthia? Cynthia!"

His wife wasn't in the bedroom, the kitchen, or the bathroom. He stumbled into the living cubicle. "Cynthia!"

She was in her TV tank. A big vat of orange gel, it held her submerged to the neck, eye-sized TV screens resting across her nose like spectacles, a twittering electric bead in each ear.

Jackson flipped up one of the screens, exposing her eye. The eye blinked and struggled to focus. The massive body twitched. "Cynthia, they're sending me outside."

"What?" She rose, dripping orange goo.

"Outside. Orders. It's an escort job."

"What are you talking about, Henry?"

He went to the closet, dragged out his combat suit, and blew some of the dust off. "They're sending me on an escort detail. Through the streets."

"Don't be ridiculous. You've made some stupid mistake."

"Orders from the President." He struggled into the suit.

"They can't *do* that, Henry! What do they think you are, some office flunky? My God, you mustn't let them— For heaven's sake, what kind of man *are* you?"

"Nothing I could do." He tucked the helmet under his arm, paused, and frowned at his wife. Was she acting genuinely surprised? A new wave of sickening suspicion spread through him. Could she and Breen have set this up between them, to get rid of Jackson? Were she and Breen having some sort of illicit *affair?* No, no, she hadn't been out of the apartment in a decade. He must try to keep his grip, what was left of it.

"Henry, you'll get killed out there!" Her voice was

trembling. She gestured agitatedly, spattering more goo. "I'm coming with you."

"No. No, this is classified. Police work."

"But . . . you're going to leave me here *all on my own?*"

He shrugged and turned the wheel of the master lock on the subapt front door. It creaked inward, shedding lumps of soot. The alarm system started whooping.

Jackson looked out into the hallway. It was the first time he'd seen it since . . . since . . . he couldn't actually remember. The bare concrete floor was covered in an inch of soft gray dust lapping up against the doors of the other subapts on this level.

"Henry!"

He turned and looked at her. "I guess you better not wait up for me," he said.

3. PARAMETERS OF THE INFRASTRUCTURE

The Chief Programmer was growing increasingly disenchanted with human beings. Everywhere he went, he had to suffer their chatter, their petty hungers, their abulia, their pathetic personal problems. Even now, comfortably cocooned in the cockpit of his personal flier, soaring through the mauve vapors of Ecozone Ten on a pleasure trip hunting big game, there was no relief.

"Heck, I've been looking forward to this trip," said ex-President of the United States R. Folsom Sullivan, sprawling in the copilot's chair.

The Chief Programmer made no reply. Ideally, he would prefer to dispense with all human beings, leaving himself the only man alive. So far, alas, he was several billion souls short of that state of grace.

He leveled off at a thousand feet, well below the top of the great geodesic dome that enclosed the Ecozone. He peered out of the side window. Game was getting scarce.

"Institutional and communications analyses were used to evaluate the public sentiments concerning the impact of the electoral scenario, you know," Sullivan said. He took out a cigar. "The people—What were their geographic and ethnic origins? Were they confined to a narrow socioeconomic stratum, or did we have a more broadly based constituency? What was their wealth index and consumer-choice profile? Yes, sir, it was a toughie." He puffed on the cigar. "See any big ugly critters out there? I feel like getting me one of them ones with the big fins and the long beak."

The Chief Programmer shook his head. "The lake's almost cleaned out. I'll tell EPA we need more radioactive waste, breed some new mutations."

The ex-President slapped his knee thoughtfully. "Yep," he said. He glanced at the Chief Programmer's firmly set jaw, his narrowed eyes, his impassive face. The Negroid features showed no trace of emotion. Sullivan had never trusted blacks, this one least of all. The Chief Programmer, working through Computer Central, had been responsible for ousting Sullivan from the White House a year ago, secretly replacing him with a mechanical look-alike. Disneyland's "Great Moments with Mr. Lincoln" had proven the practicality of the scheme.

The real Sullivan had not backed down gracefully. But he had been forced to face that he was not really in charge anymore, anyway. Computer Central had long since taken over most of the functions of government, in America and the rest of the world. What was the sense of maintaining a human President as a figurehead, liable to make embarrassing blunders and impulsive decisions that could foul up Central's carefully optimized global scenario?

So Sullivan had been banished to secret offices buried in the Rocky Mountains, where he wrote endless memos and worked on his autobiography. An occasional hunting trip was his only recreation.

"Killed anything yet, hon?" The Chief Programmer's companion, Charlotte, emerged from the cabin into the cockpit and rested her long, manicured hand tenderly on the shoulder of the man to whom her every waking moment was devoted. "Gee, it looks kinda murky out there."

Charlotte was nubile, big-breasted, petite, and blond, with a wanton, adoring demeanor. Like Sullivan's double in the White House, she was a robot. But whereas the mechanical President required only two expressions (a beneficent smile and a frown of grave concern), Charlotte could pout, kiss, moan, and mimic every emotional resonance. While the President had a limited range of movements (he could sit, stand, walk slowly, shake hands, and scratch his head in an endearing, boyish fashion), Charlotte could belly dance, cook coq au vin, and play the dulcimer. In contrast to the President, who spoke like a ventriloquist's dummy in response to coded radio commands from Computer Central, Charlotte had a self-contained vocabulary of several thousand words and could respond to simple verbal cues from human companions. She was devoted to the hunched little gnome of a man who had created her, and frequently reminded people of his humble origins as a token black at IBM who had worked his way up to virtual world domination with only his native wit and determination to aid him.

The Chief Programmer guided the flier into a dense bank of black clouds near the center of the dome, and turned the flier's lights on. Oily droplets snaked across the windows. "Aha! There's one for you, boy."

Sullivan peered forward. "What? Where?"

"Looks like a neopterodactyl. A fifty-footer. Amazing how they stay in the air." Admiration flickered across the Chief Programmer's face as the big bird came clearly into view. "Carrying enough industrial mercury to decimate a dozen day-care centers. They feed off phosphates, you know." He circled closer to the bird.

"I'll use the gun," said Sullivan, moving from the

cockpit to an observation bubble. He squinted through the gunsight, his teeth clenched on his cigar. He pressed the fire button. There was a whoosh and a muffled thump as a missile was launched into the bird and a giant net under the flier scooped it out of the air.

Sullivan returned to the copilot's chair. "Direct hit," he said, pleased with himself.

"Congratulations," said the Chief Programmer. The projectiles were, of course, self-aiming. The sole purpose of this trip was to humor Sullivan, in case his look-alike in Washington ever malfunctioned or Computer Central went offline. In that case, the real Sullivan would be rushed back into office while repairs were made. For the time being, it was necessary to keep him alive and cooperative, even though this entailed a certain amount of aggravation.

Sullivan relit his cigar. "Expect any trouble at the World Council next week?" he remarked. "I hear the upcoming scenario from Central is gonna be a biggie."

The Chief Programmer shrugged. "I try not to look ahead, boy."

"Horse shit. You have the parameters of the infrastructure. You sure as hell know which way the ball's gonna bounce. You and that cellarful of radio parts."

"Computer Central wouldn't like to hear you talk about it like that."

Sullivan glanced around uneasily as if half expecting to find a concealed microphone. "Well, anyhow"—he lowered his voice—"can it save the planet?"

"Even I am not informed in advance of Central's plans," the Chief Programmer lied smoothly, taking the flier in a wide arc and turning toward home. "But as you say, the prime objective is to save the world. Am I right?"

"Why, hon, you're always right," said Charlotte, massaging the back of her mentor's neck.

"And speaking of *robots*," said Sullivan, drumming his fingers on the armrest and pointedly staring straight ahead, "I hear that fool thing of yours, the one you built on the Moon a while ago, has been let loose. Isn't that what's running around New York today? I heard on the federal network news this morning—''

"What exactly did they say?" the Chief Programmer interrupted sharply.

"Just some baloney about field-testing a new kind of crime-control device for citizen safety."

"Good. That was the story we gave them."

"Guess you fooled those saps," said Sullivan, "but you didn't pull the wool over my eyes. Soon as they said it was indistinguishable from a human being, I remembered when you snuck that gizmo into the defense budget. Seem to recall I was in the Oval Office at the time." He drifted off for a moment, staring glumly at tendrils of red and purple gas streaming past the cockpit window. "Anyhow," he went on, "I thought you had that gadget locked in a government lab someplace."

The Chief Programmer sighed. Sullivan's thirst for petty gossip was a constant distraction. "The psych people gave up on Bertha," he said. "Some kind of amnesia. And because the brain is totally organic, there was no way they could strip it down for tests. They spent six months on it, then decided the only thing to do was turn it loose and watch what happens."

"Yes, but what's the darn thing *for?* You never did explain."

"Pure research. It's not *for* anything."

Sullivan leaned over and tapped the Chief Programmer on the shoulder. "Listen, son, you can hornswoggle John Q. Public, but sure as shit, *I* know you didn't requisition a trillion dollars without being pret-ty darned sure of getting something in return."

The Chief Programmer glanced with distaste at the intrusive, prodding finger. "Mr. Sullivan, you forget yourself." A muscle twitched in his cheek. "Charlotte," he said, "perhaps you could entertain Mr. Sullivan in the back for a while."

"Why sure, hon." She gave Sullivan a lascivious wink. "You come on along with me."

"Hell, no!" Sullivan stood up clumsily. He waved his fat hand as if to hold her away from him.

"You prefer to relax in the cabin on your own?" the Chief Programmer suggested blandly.

"Fine," said Sullivan. "Mighty fine. I'll do just that." He left the cockpit, slamming the door behind him.

The Chief Programmer absentmindedly fondled the life-like flesh of his synthetic companion. She squirmed realistically, and he glanced up at her with genuine affection. There had to be a solution to the human condition, he mused. Preferably, some kind of final solution.

Beneath the flier, huge mutant fish churned through the sludge that had once been Lake Michigan. Since all attempts had failed to diminish society's outpouring of garbage and industrial waste, Computer Central's logical answer had been to contain the effluents in limited areas. This one was now almost full; best choice for Ecozone Eleven was the Grand Canyon. It would be a simple roofing-over job.

4. THE NEEDY AND THE GREEDY

"Hey, cute little lady! Hey, I got 'em, you want 'em?"

Melanie ignored the guttural voice shouting to her above the babble of the East 42nd Street bazaar—the cries of street traders, bawling of babies, yapping of dogs in the meat pen, honking horns of pedmobiles, blaring of cheap radios. She squinted against gusts of soot and fumes and felt her resolve weaken.

But she couldn't bear to go crawling back to her father and his community of long-haired degenerates. She tightened her grip on her portable phonograph and her baby blue travel case. If she could just get as far as the midtown Safe Zone and catch one of the express buses to the community soup kitchens of Yonkers, or even Pleasantville—

"Hey, little lady! I got 'em right here!" A stooped, hairy, filth-encrusted hobo was wheeling a rusty supermarket shopping cart toward her, picking his way between lumps of masonry that had fallen from the surrounding skyscrapers. One bloodshot eye leered at Melanie from behind strands of hair caked in mud. "Tasty!" he said, and smacked his lips.

Melanie realized she couldn't afford to hesitate any longer in the doorway of the Chrysler Building. Her pristine clothes and air of innocence would attract altogether the wrong sort of attention. She started forward, then recoiled with a cry of dismay as the old man blocked her way with his cart and she saw its cargo. It was full of rats wriggling and fighting one another and trying to climb out from under a scrap of chicken wire that turned the cart into a mobile cage.

"I kill one for you right now," the hobo offered. He slid a gloved hand into the cart and expertly seized a fat black rat by the tail. He pulled it out and dangled it enticingly in front of her. It writhed and squealed, baring yellow fangs. "Look at this little beauty. Caught 'im fresh last night down in Grand Central. Tasty! For you, little lady, ten bucks."

Melanie backed away, torn between revulsion and pity. What sort of a world was it (she asked herself) where pathetic old men must tramp the streets in all weathers, selling rats to eke out meager State Food rations? "I can't help you," she blurted. "I'm sorry, I truly am!"

He cocked his head to one side. "I take State Credit."

"No, no, please, leave me alone." Melanie shook her head, making her blond curls bob. She backed away from the man, clutching her possessions.

He threw the rat back in with the others and started after her. "Hey, I got other shit. How's about some *beef fat,* huh? Found it in a trash compactor on Fiftieth and Second. It's fresh, I swear to God, lady.''

Melanie dropped her possessions and put her hands over her ears. "God! How can you talk of God in a world like this!'' Her chest was aching and her eyes were burning from the fumes that laced the air. She started to cry.

"Hey, lady, no offense.'' The old man parked his cart and edged closer. "I didn't know as how you're a Christian.'' He reached to touch her arm, thought better of it, and reached for her suitcase instead.

Melanie grabbed the case. "No! This and my phonograph are all I own in the *whole world!*''

She swallowed hard, trying to get her emotions under control. Already her encounter with the hobo had been noticed by others on the street. The place was swarming with peasant people, in and around shacks built from discarded desks and file cabinets littering the highway and sidewalks. A rag man was greedily studying her freshly pressed pleated plaid skirt with its big safety pin, and her blindingly white bobby sox. A pimp had parked his customized pedmobile and was sauntering toward her with a wide, gap-toothed grin. Two teenagers in wastepaper loincloths were skipping barefoot through the rubble, moving to music only they could hear, homing in on her hungrily. One of them was reaching for a machete in a sheath at his hip.

There was no point in shouting for help: the vigilantes had long since given up patrolling this neighborhood. Melanie quickly wiped her eyes with her monogrammed lace handkerchief, staining it with soot and mascara. She grabbed her suitcase in one hand and her Dansette portable phonograph in the other, and turned and ran toward Third Avenue.

She heard shouts and catcalls from behind her. Startled faces stared out at her from makeshift cardboard huts and shanties along the curb. Others peered down from windows of what had once been office buildings and were now refugee camps for the peps who had been relocated in derelict areas of Manhattan and left to fend for themselves.

Melanie slipped on rotting garbage that had been thrown

from the upper stories, and almost fell. She glanced over her shoulder and saw that the crowd of street people was coming after her. Worst of all, no sanctuary lay ahead: the nearest business district was behind her on Fifth Avenue.

Her pert breasts bobbed under her pink cardigan, her penny loafers went pitter-pat over the rubble, and the rank air rasped in and out of her lungs. She was running as fast as she could, yet the mob was gaining on her. They were acclimatized to the unfiltered smog. It was all her father's fault. If only—

She never completed the thought. As she reached Third Avenue, a 1966 Oldsmobile Toronado appeared without warning and pulled up in front of her at the curb.

Melanie stopped and stared. A big, old-fashioned, gasoline-burning car in New York City?

The driver got out. He was a 40-year-old hoodlum in black motorcycle boots, tight jeans, and a black leather jacket with WILD ANGEL hand-painted in red across his shoulders. He grinned at her, chewing gum, and idly ran a comb through his well-oiled black hair, as if he had time to kill. Then he reached in his car, pulled out a small oxygen cylinder, and tossed it to her. "Seems like you could use some, kid," he said laconically, hooking his thumbs in his belt.

"Oh, thank you!" Melanie gasped, pressing the rubber mask to her face.

"Take your time. I'll see they don't bother you none," the stranger said, eyeing the street people. They were still advancing, but more cautiously now, staring at the vintage car with the same wide-eyed disbelief that Melanie had shown.

She took another deep breath of oxygen. It didn't smell the same as the brand she was used to. And somehow it wasn't clearing her head. In fact, she was feeling more and more giddy. She gave a little cry; the world was fragmenting in bright colors, as though she were falling into a kaleidoscope.

She looked at the leather-jacketed hoodlum with sudden realization. "Drugged . . . oxygen!" she gasped.

"Yeah, nice, huh?" He grinned and caught the tank as it slid from her fingers. He threw it into his automobile, then guided Melanie into the passenger seat as her knees buckled under her. He tossed her possessions in the back, jumped in, and slammed the door. The mob cried out in anger, suddenly realizing that their prize was being stolen from them. They surged forward and started hammering on the car with their fists.

The leather-jacketed punk made an obscene gesture at the contorted faces pressed against the Soft-Ray tinted glass. Then he revved the motor, threw the transmission into Drive, and the car surged forward, abducting Melanie to a destination unknown.

5. SCIENTIFIC HARDWARE

The elevator made ominous grinding noises as it carried Henry Jackson toward the surface. No one normally used it, because no one went outside anymore—not in Jackson's income bracket, anyway. You had to be crazy to visit "ground zero," as subapt dwellers called the outside world, with a mixture of fear and loathing. Crazy, or *victimized*, Jackson thought bitterly.

He donned his protective helmet, grunting with the effort of moving his arms. His combat suit fit him like an old-time astronaut's space suit. Its power unit was dead, so none of the servomotors was working. Unfair; it was all unfair.

The elevator shuddered to a halt and the doors squeaked open. Jackson staggered out into a drab concrete vestibule

lit by a single glow panel. He remembered it from . . .
when? Years ago, one Sunday morning, Cynthia had nagged
him to go out and buy her some bagels from the little store
in Harlem Park, back in the days when bagels still existed,
and the old park still existed, and money still existed,
honest-to-God paper money.

Jackson shuffled though the dust to the first set of
armored steel exit doors, muttered his identification code
into the recognition unit, and waited while the doors slid
open. Apprehension was gathering like iced water in his
bowels. The second, final set of doors lay just ahead.
Jackson tightened the air filter across his mouth and nose.

The outer doors opened, he stepped through—and recoiled
in shock. Glaring sunlight smote him in the face, so bright
it seemed to beam straight into the quivering pulp of his
brain. And it was . . . it was . . . for a moment he
couldn't think of the word. Hot! It was *hot!*

His eyes were streaming tears, unaccustomed to anything stronger than a 40-watt glow tube. Sweat was breaking out under the confines of his suit.

"Good morning, Chief."

Jackson wheeled around clumsily. He tripped over his
own boots and fell backward, his shoulders slamming into
the armored doors that had closed automatically behind
him.

"The weather is fine, eh, Chief?"

Jackson screwed up his eyes against the glare. He saw a
combat-suited cop with an armored pedmobile parked in
the street behind him. "Who the hell are you?" he gasped.

"Sergeant Sanchez, Chief. You remember me, we talk
on the fone once in a while."

"Maybe I've seen someone who looks like you," Jackson answered warily. He wrestled with one of the pockets
of his suit, finally wrenched it open, and dragged out his
compad. "What's your first name, Sanchez? And your
Social Security number."

"No, Chief, we don't got time for all that, they waiting
for us in headquarters for the escort detail."

"Just give me the goddamn facts!" Jackson fumbled with

the compad's stylus in his armor-gloved hand and started stabbing buttons. The display promptly filled with cryptic, flickering symbols. Malfunctioning, he hadn't used it in years. Overwhelmed with sudden fury, Jackson threw the thing down, drew his gun, and fired two rounds into it.

The recoil slammed the pistol grip painfully into the palm of his hand. The explosions were frighteningly loud. He cringed as bullets ricocheted off the concrete paving. Echoes of the gunshots died slowly away.

"Just come this way, eh, Chief?" Sanchez tactfully guided Jackson by the arm.

"Sorry I was a little rough with you back there," Jackson said later, sitting beside Sergeant Sanchez in the gun turret of the pedmobile. It was heading south through the remains of Harlem Park, toward midtown, its cleated tracks crunching through debris that littered the highway. "I just don't believe in taking any chances, understand?"

"Sure, Chief." Sanchez had a smooth, expressionless face, with a Zapata mustache that concealed most of his mouth. He spoke quietly, easily, as if nothing troubled him.

Jackson's eyes narrowed. He had never trusted Hispanics—or any other non-Caucasian ethnic group, for that matter. He wondered if Sanchez was the one who had set him up for this job. That was a distinct possibility.

"You know, one time I live in this part of town," Sanchez was saying. "When I am a kid, and the buildings are still in Harlem, remember that time?"

"Slums," Jackson muttered, half listening. "Whole place was a stinking, vermin-infested slum in those days."

"But they pull down all the buildings and they make it into Harlem Park," Sanchez went on, "for all the rich people in the new fancy underground apartments." He looked at Jackson and grinned, teeth flashing white.

"Damn right," Jackson agreed. "Cleaned it all up. But now look at it!" He gestured through the observation slit. Peasant people had long since invaded the park and seized the land. Emaciated women and children were toiling in rice paddies and soybean plantations either side of the road. "My God, Sanchez, I used to walk my wife's poodle in this park! I used to sit here and view *The Wall Street Journal* on my portable modem, till the goddam peps moved in."

"Hm, too bad," Sanchez said noncommittally.

"I'll say it's too bad. The stinking United Revolutionary Party of Oppressed Third World Peoples . . . Know what I'd do if I was running this town, Sanchez? Nuke it."

"You nuke Manhattan?" Sergeant Sanchez raised his eyebrows fractionally.

"Correct! Most decent, God-fearing, tax-paying American citizens live in nuke-proof subapts, right? You do yourself, right? So we'd just pick off the scum."

Sanchez shook his head. "Be bad for me, you blow it up when I am on duty."

Jackson wasn't listening. He grabbed the handles of the laser cannon in front of him and peered through the rangefinder, baring his teeth. "C'mon, Sanchez, let's hot-beam some gooks right now."

"Hey, Chief, careful with that thing, man!"

"Crank it." Jackson nodded at the hand-powered generator beside the weapon. "Just gimme enough charge for a ten-second burst. I remember one time in Vietnam—"

"That is a while back, Chief. You know it was different then." Sanchez let go the pedmobile's steering wheel for a moment and apologetically pried Jackson's hand from the cannon's pistol grip. "Here is a democracy. The people got rights."

"The greatest good for the greatest number," Jackson muttered, as if the words tasted foul. He slumped back in his seat. "Tyranny of the mob." He brooded silently for a moment. "So how come they sent a goddam pedmobile to pick me up?"

"The steam cars all on patrol, Chief. What's wrong, this don't go fast enough? I get the guys to pedal harder." He gestured toward the floor, beneath which the labored breathing of ten sweating men and the rhythmic squeak-squeak of pedals were faintly audible.

"I don't give a damn how fast we get there," said Jackson. "Tomorrow would be too soon, if you want my candid opinion, Sergeant. I simply feel a man of my rank deserves better. In fact, this whole assignment is an insult." He broke off, realizing he was talking too freely. Why was Sanchez asking so many questions? How much did this wetback know, anyway?

Sanchez guided the pedmobile out of Harlem Park, leaving behind the barbed-wire fences and guard towers erected by the farmers to protect their crops. The vehicle continued south down Fifth Avenue.

"Another neighborhood gone to hell," Jackson muttered. "My father used to own a condo on this block, till the crash of '95."

"What happen to him?"

"Wiped out. All his stock was in IBM and General Motors. He had a heart attack, they took him to Bellevue, but the emergency room attendants were on strike, they wouldn't touch him."

"Too bad," said Sanchez.

"Damn right it's *too bad*. So now there's a dope-smoking pervert squatting in my old dad's penthouse, committing sex crimes with some festering runaway twelve-year-old hooker."

Sanchez shook his head. "No, the poets, the artists, the people like that live in this part of town now."

Jackson laughed derisively. "You fall for that? You, a New York City cop? Cut the crap, Sanchez. If these people were real artists, real writers, they'd be working in television or advertising and making a respectable living. You and I know they're nothing but a bunch of social parasites."

They sat in silence through most of the rest of the drive, till the pedmobile reached the checkpoint and guard post at the edge of the Safe Zone. Here, at last, Jackson could relax. There were respectably dressed citizens on the streets (though he noticed disapprovingly that some of them were black). Steam-powered, sleek Japanese robot cops trundled to and fro, their scanners busily monitoring the environment for any sign of crime. The situation was entirely under control.

The pedmobile made a right on 53rd Street and stopped outside midtown police headquarters, in the big glass tower that had once been the New York Hilton.

"So where's this, this *robot?*" Jackson asked as Sanchez helped him down from the gun turret.

"They hold him in the lobby. This way, Chief."

Jackson felt a wave of nostalgia when he saw the familiar dented gray armor plate lining the walls, ceiling, and floor of the lobby. Ten years ago, he'd been in charge of the renovation project that had converted the guest rooms into maximum-security cells and the ground floor and basement into administrative offices. It had been his last surface assignment, and he was proud of it. Even now, so far as he knew, no one had ever escaped from the Hilton.

The lobby was in its usual state of uproar. At one end, an unruly mob of peps besieged the robot admission clerk, jabbering at it in a dozen languages, pleading to visit their jailbird relatives. The clerk's speech circuits had overloaded, and its defense system kept throwing high-voltage jolts into the crowd. Jackson noticed with some satisfaction that several ragged figures had been zapped unconscious and were now being trampled underfoot.

At the other end of the lobby, cops were bringing in suspects with cattle prods, billy clubs, and steel-mesh nets. And in one corner, guarded by a platoon of New York's Finest, stood a tall young man in a white hospital gown. He was watching the lobby scene with strange, wide eyes.

"Him, he is the robot," said Sanchez. "Bertha, they call him."

Jackson's boots clanged over the stained metal floor. "A trillion dollars," he muttered, shaking his head in bafflement.

The nearest cops recognized him and stood to attention, more or less. Several were chewing gum, one of them was watching a pocket TV, and a couple at the back were playing cards. Jackson scowled. If he had his way . . . but

why bother? The main thing was to live through this
assignment and get back underground as quickly as possible.

"All right, you," he called to the robot. "I'm Chief of
Police Henry Jackson, and I'm taking you into my custody."

The white-robed man's dreamy blue eyes focused on
Jackson. He smiled, leaned forward between the cops, and
extended his hand. "My pleasure is to meet you," he said.
His voice sounded oddly melodic against the background
din.

Jackson hesitated. He wasn't going to shake hands with
a *thing*. "So I understand you want to wander around
town," he said gruffly.

"I have been looking forward to it."

Jackson eyed the robot skeptically. He was beginning to
wonder if this was some kind of double con. It didn't look
synthetic. It looked like your average everyday human
screwball or kook. Back when Jackson had been a patrolman, he'd seen weirdos like that hanging around the park,
talking to themselves in Greek, and exposing themselves
to little girls.

"So how do we know you're a robot?" he demanded.

The man in white started unbuttoning his robe. *Hah!
Just as I figured,* Jackson thought to himself, *the guy's a
flasher.*

But he only opened the robe as far as his stomach.
"You see, Mr. Jackson?" he said, still with the strange
smile.

Jackson peered at the exposed pink skin. No navel. Not
a trace. Well, that was some sort of proof, though he
wasn't sure exactly how much. "All right," he said wearily. "Where do you want to go?"

"A place where there are implements of metal, and
plant fiber derivatives," said the man in white, rebuttoning
his clothes.

"Jesus Christ," Jackson muttered, vowing further ven-
geance on whoever had done this to him. "What do you
mean, a—a restaurant?"

"No! I do not wish to eat. I wish to make something."

"Perhaps he mean a hardware store," said Sanchez.

"That is correct!" The man's face lit up with pleasure. "Hardware!" The word seemed to have some sort of mystical significance.

"All right, let's go. You men, put away that deck of cards." Jackson turned to Sanchez. "Where the hell can we find a hardware store in midtown? And what do you figure this kook is liable to do when we get there?"

"On Third Avenue, I think, maybe," Sanchez said dubiously.

"But . . . that's outside the Safe Zone!"

Sanchez shrugged and spread his hands.

Clever, Jackson thought to himself. Very clever. Just a poor dumb Puerto Rican, right? Well, there was only one way to find out. "All right, Third Avenue. Let's go."

People on the sidewalk stopped and stared at the police platoon in combat suits shepherding the weirdo in the white gown.

"Clouds!" said the man in white, pointing at the sky with delight. "White, blue, and gray! Glass buildings! I am happy!"

"I'd like to find the federal bureaucrat who pissed away the taxpayers' money on this," Jackson said to no one in particular. He grabbed the robot's arm. "Come on, you."

"I am already coming along," he answered, looking surprised. "It is good to be outside. For a long time, they kept me inside."

"I can see why," said Jackson.

They headed across town, ignoring the stares from passersby. Fifth Avenue marked the eastern edge of the safe business district; Jackson saw the garbage, filth, and human detritus of shantytown ahead. "Sanchez, tell your men to have their weapons ready, and don't hesitate to use them."

"You hear the Chief," said Sanchez.

The armed phalanx marched past the guard post, into the ghetto zone. Street people turned and stared, and some started shouting abuse. "They are talking to us!" the man in white exclaimed. "Hello, people!" he called happily, and waved. "Nice day!"

"Keep your head down, dummy," said Jackson, although,

to his relief, the peps hadn't started throwing things, hadn't turned into a mob. Most were going about their business. Still, the tension was taking its toll. Jackson's muscles felt like jelly, and he was sweating so much he seemed to be swimming in his suit.

"This is the place," said Sanchez after they had walked several blocks.

"Right," said Jackson. "You and me and the robot will go in while your men stand guard outside."

The hardware store was tiny, crammed with locks, iron bars, gates, weapons, bulletproof clothing, and lethal defense systems. The old proprietor perched on a stool behind the counter, which was walled in with steel mesh and salvaged Lucite. "Help you gennelmen?" he called through a loudspeaker.

Jackson glanced around. The place looked okay, but you could never be sure. He scrutinized Sanchez. If this was a setup, Sanchez was being pretty damned cool about it. He turned to the store owner. "I'm Henry Jackson, Chief of Police." He fumbled in his suit and brought out his ID badge. "This—man—is in our custody. Sell him whatever he wants, and bill the city."

"The city." The man looked dubious.

"You will get paid," Sanchez reassured him.

"Glad to help you gennelmen." He coughed and spat, and glared at them wearily.

"Good, I am glad too," said the man in the robe. He started poking around in the display racks, giving occasional little cries of excitement.

"So hurry it up," Jackson complained.

"No hurry, I have everything." He selected several items and took them over to the counter.

The proprietor started punching product codes into an ancient inventory computer. "Screwdriver, can of spackle, six-foot extension cord, ball of nylon string, electric-candle neon light bulb, digital alarm clock. That be all, gennelmen? Sign here, please." He pushed a digitablet through a slit in his protective cubicle.

Jackson scrawled his name, then grabbed the arm of the

man in white. "All right, you want all this crap, you carry
it. Let's go."

"No, I do not carry it, it carries me. Wait." He swiftly
used his teeth to chop and strip the extension cord, then
deftly braided the copper wire into a misshapen knot. He
stuck the neon bulb in the center, then used the screwdriver to pry the lid off the can of spackle and the back
off the digital clock. He daubed spackle on the base of the
light bulb, then quickly pushed the ends of the wire inside
the clock.

"Let's go already!" Jackson complained, tugging at the
robot's arm.

"Yes, I will go now." He bit off a length of nylon
string, looped it under his arms, and knotted it quickly so
that the tangled wire and digital clock were tied to his
chest. Then he gave Jackson a happy grin.

"You're a nut," said Jackson.

Sanchez was by the door. He was looking unhappy.
"We got a problem, Chief."

"Those peps? They give us any trouble, you tell your
men it's time to fry some flesh."

"No, Chief, you don't understand. My men, they are
the problem. They disappear."

"What?" Jackson stepped out onto the empty sidewalk.
He looked up and down the block. There wasn't a cop in
sight.

"Is not my fault they run away," Sanchez said, looking
worried.

"Not your *fault?*" Jackson's voice rose from a whine to
a squawk. "What kind of dummy do you think I am? You
think I got where I am letting spics like you play me for a
sucker? Mister, you're under arrest." He pulled out his
gun. He was shaking so badly he needed both hands to
hold it.

"Chief, look behind you."

"Oh, come *on,* Sanchez! You expect me to fall for that?"

"But behind you, Chief, the robot, he is getting away."

Jackson hesitated, then turned in genuine panic. The
man in white was wandering off into the shantytown of

Third Avenue. "Hey you!" Jackson shouted. "Freeze!" He pointed his gun, then realized what would happen if he pulled the trigger. He imagined the headlines: trillion-dollar robot blown away by killer cop.

He holstered his gun and started lumbering forward in his combat suit. "Come back here, you!"

The man in white turned around. "No, I must go now," he said with seeming regret. "But thank you so much."

"Hey, what are you doing with that crap?"

"Antigravity, I think." He was fiddling with the digital clock in the tangle of wires on his chest. Suddenly the neon bulb lit up. "Yes. My memory is so bad. Good-bye!" The nylon string tightened under his arms. Slowly, the misshapen assembly started lifting him into the air.

"No!" Jackson's voice was a horrified wail echoing up and down the street. He stumbled forward as the robot drifted upward. He made a despairing leap, tried to clutch the robot's ankles, but missed by several yards. He fell backward like a spastic spaceman. The last thing he saw was a fire hydrant, an instant before his head slammed into it.

Behind him, outside the hardware store, Sergeant Sanchez shaded his eyes, watching the robot fly away. He pulled out his comm unit. "This is Bertha robot escort detail, Third Avenue Fifty-third Street, Sergeant Sanchez. Come in, please." The comm unit gave a squawk of acknowledgment. "The men run away and leave me here with Mr. Jackson. The robot fly into the sky. Yes, he escape. Mr. Jackson fall down and hit his head. No, he not look so good. Send ambulance. Yes, Third and Fifty-third. I know is not a good neighborhood, but you send anyway, ten-four?"

He waited for an acknowledgment, then put the comm unit away.

"Too bad," he said, shaking his head.

6. ENDSVILLE

Sunlight played on Melanie's eyelids. Seagulls were crying, and Elvis was singing "Love Me Tender."

Melanie opened her eyes and found herself lying on her back, outside in the open air. She blinked, feeling disoriented, and then she remembered being abducted by the hoodlum on Third Avenue, and she sat up in panic.

For a moment, she couldn't understand what she saw. She was on some strange sort of couch with buttons and levers and dials beside the armrests, and wires dangling from panels either side. Behind her rustled the faded fronds of a plastic palm tree. To her left a genuine AMI jukebox was playing Elvis on a vintage 45. All around her were huge piles of mechanical junk: refrigerators, TV sets, cooking stoves, automobile parts, radios, everything at least forty years old.

She slid off the couch and found that her legs were shaky, but she could stand. She saw she was on a rooftop patio, outside the sliding glass doors of a penthouse apartment. She picked her way through the mounds of junk, reached the balcony rail, and discovered with a shock that for the first time in her young life she was no longer in Manhattan. The turgid brown waters of the East River lay between her and the towers of midtown. Peasant people were fishing from sampans in the shadow of the 59th Street Bridge, its collapsed girders lying half-submerged, dotted with seagulls and slime. "Why, this must be Roosevelt Island," she said to herself.

"Endsville, doll," said a voice from behind her. "Least-
ways, that's what I call it."

Melanie turned quickly as the hoodlum in the leather
jacket stepped out of the apartment and onto the patio. She
saw a tire iron lying among the surplus auto parts nearby.
She quickly picked it up, and held it menacingly.

"Hey, take it easy!" He held up his hands in defense.
"I don't mean you no harm."

"Then why did you trick me that way? Why did you
bring me to this place?" She hoped he couldn't see how
scared she felt.

"Had to pull you out any way I could." He brushed his
long black hair away from his forehead. He had a wide,
tanned face, a square jaw, dark eyes with crinkles at the
corners. His voice was deep and he spoke slowly, easily.
"Those peps would've stomped you for sure."

"You didn't have to drug me."

"Wouldn't have got you in my car any other way.
Wasn't no time to argue, doll. Hey, look, you want to cut
out, you go right ahead. Take your stuff along—See, I put
it right there." He gestured at her suitcase and phonograph
standing beside the jukebox.

Melanie realized it was true that he had saved her, and
he didn't seem to have interfered with her possessions, and
he seemed not to have molested her while she was unconscious (so far as she could tell) . . . but he had deceived
her, nonetheless. "I don't see how you can expect me to
trust you," she said, lowering the tire iron but still keeping
hold of it.

"Hey, you don't have to trust me, or not trust me, or
anything." He gave her a wide, easy grin and brushed his
hair back again. "But I'd sure like it better if you put
another record on the jukebox."

Elvis had finished crooning, and the music had died.
Melanie had never actually seen a real jukebox before. She
risked a quick glance at the list of selections. Her eyes
widened in disbelief. "You have all these records here?"

"Pick any one you like, sweetheart."

"But I didn't think anyone else in the world still lis-

tened to these wonderful songs!'' She looked back at him
with new interest.

"Funny, I thought I was the only one till I saw you on
the street with your '56 Dansette autochanger. I thought, I
could get killed going in after this chick, but looks like
she's a hepcat same as me, so I took a chance." He pulled
a pack of Juicy Fruit out of the top pocket of his jacket and
took out a stick. He grinned again. ''Want some?''

"Well, I . . . I guess I do." Shyly, Melanie put down
the tire iron. She took a piece of gum from him, being
careful, still, not to move too close. Her eyes met his and
she felt herself blush. "I can pick any song I like?"

"Of course."

She punched buttons for Roy Orbison's "Only the
Lonely." How often she had dreamed of meeting someone
who understood and cared for the same things that mattered to her. She stole another quick glance at him. If only
he weren't so old! At least forty, she judged. "What's
your name?" she asked.

"Mick. And you?"

"Melanie. Um, do you—that is, may I use your bathroom?" She urgently needed to check her makeup, and
she was sure her hair must need combing and spraying.

"Down the hall," he said, gesturing through the doors
to his apartment. He watched her retrieve her suitcase and
pick her way daintily across the littered patio. "So you,
uh, ain't gonna make tracks outa here, huh?"

He sounded less self-assured than before, and Melanie
wondered if he had been feeling isolated all these years,
just like her. "I only want to freshen up," she assured
him.

He nodded. "Well, the place is kind of a mess. I'm into
antiques, know what I mean? I find things and fix 'em.
Hey, you want lunch? I could cook us some soyburgers,
and I got a couple bottles of vintage Coke, the real thing.
What do you say?"

"Why, I—I'd appreciate that." She blushed again and
avoided his eyes, trying not to let him see how much the
idea excited her.

"Here you go," he said, taking her elbow and helping her over a heap of hubcaps half blocking the doorway. The living room beyond was stacked to the ceiling with pinball machines, old tires, guitar amplifiers, movie posters, tools, telephones, motorcycle engines, reel-to-reel tape recorders, and all kinds of other junk. "Just down the hall. Second door on the left."

"Thanks," she said. "I'll be right back."

When she returned to the patio, she found Mick had set fire to some driftwood under a barbecue grill and was putting raffia place mats on an aluminum picnic table. "So, uh, how come you're stuck on the fifties?" he asked her as she settled herself demurely on a bent-metal patio chair that he had painstakingly repainted in its original flamingo pink.

"Because in those days people did what was right," she said, choosing her words carefully. "They went on romantic dates in beautiful automobiles, they exchanged vows and loved each other and their children in split-level suburban homes, they drove to church every Sunday, and they worked hard and supported their government and made lots of money."

"Oh. Uh-huh." He frowned and dumped a couple of the soyburgers on the grill. They sizzled appetizingly. "I guess I don't know too much about that. I just dig the, you know, the style."

"There is more to life than style, Mick," she said, frowning at him. "I hope you know the difference between right and wrong."

"I never done time for nothing, if that's what you're saying."

Melanie sighed. He did seem a basically good person, but terribly naive. She decided she should try to enlighten him a little. She started telling him about her life in the Chrysler Building Commune: the free love, pagan rituals, drug abuse, and unhygienic habits. "Those people were degenerates, Mick. Life among them was a nightmare for me."

"Yeah, I can see as how you'd want to get the hell

out,'' he agreed, serving the burgers with genuine ketchup and Wonder Bread buns. He checked the Coke for sediment. then applied the back of a church-key opener and slipped a candy-striped straw into each bottle, just the way she'd seen it in the ads in old romance magazines.

"This is just wonderful," she said, taking a dainty sip and savoring it. "It's very kind of you." She nibbled the burger. "Won't you tell me about yourself?"

He explained that he'd grown up in this apartment with his parents. His father was a race-car driver, unemployable after the gasoline shortages of the 1990s and the government rationing that followed. His parents had jumped into the Verrazano Narrows with thousands of others in the mass suicides on New Year's Eve, 1999. Mick had retreated into a life of solitude, surrounding himself with icons from the past that recaptured the life his father had led, back in the decades when power had been plentiful and plastic cheap.

"But then the FALN blew up the Fifty-ninth Street Bridge, and the cable car stopped running, so there wasn't no way the State Food deliveries could get over here. Ain't more than a couple dozen people living on the island these days. Just some bums in Fun City—you know, the entertainment center, couple blocks from here. I take 'em food once in a while. Crazy old guys. Too crazy to leave. I fixed up some of the rides over there too, for something to do. Used to go there when I was a kid.''

"But how do *you* survive?" Melanie asked.

"Well, I welded up some sheet steel, made myself a raft. Just big enough for me and the car. See, I found a gasoline dump nobody else knows about. Couple hundred gallons the feds left when they pulled out ten years back. I do a run into Wall Street once a week, trading oxygen. No, not the drugged stuff, that's just for self-defense.''

"But selling oxygen without a license is illegal!"

He looked at her blankly. "What you going to do, turn me in? Look, I deal clean gas. Got a compressor and a freezer in the apartment downstairs. I filter it, I use good tanks, it's better than the legitimate stuff.''

Melanie finished her burger and laid her fork neatly across her plate. She sighed. "I suppose it isn't really your fault. Society has driven you to live outside the law. Oh, if only we were living fifty years ago! Life was so wonderful then!"

"Ain't that the truth." He tilted his chair back and studied her with his dark, compelling eyes. "Think about it. We'd bop at the hop, race hot rods, go surfing; maybe I'd treat you to a drive-in movie."

Melanie nodded. She bit her lip. He had been so kind to her, and she hated to hurt his feelings, but there was something she simply had to say. She stood up, went to the jukebox, and put on Paul Anka's "Diana."

"Mick," she said, clasping her hands nervously, "you're tops, and you have a terrific personality, but I don't think you're quite right for me. It's nothing personal, just that . . . just that I'm so young and you're so old."

He reached in his motorcycle boot, pulled out a switch-blade, and used it to scrape the remnants off the dishes. "Had a feeling that was what you was going to say."

"But we can still be friends, can't we?"

"Well, sure. Anyhow, you're right, you're too young. I think maybe I need like an older woman who actually lived back then. Know what I mean? She could teach me all kinds of things." His eyes took on a distant, dreamy look.

"That sounds nice, Mick." She sat down at the table again. "Just as long as you won't hold it against me that we can't go steady."

He replaced the knife in his boot and shook his head. "I already got a heap of romance." He reached for a rusty ammunition box lying nearby, opened it, pulled out a bunch of yellowing magazines, and tossed them on the table. "See what I mean?"

"True Heart Throbs! My favorite! And I've never seen this one!" She grabbed them eagerly.

"I got a couple hundred of 'em," he said. "You better make yourself comfortable on the G-couch there—yeah, the thing you was on when you woke up. I bought it off of a guy claimed he used to be an astronaut back when. Said he kept it for sentimental value.''

"But what are you going to do?" Melanie asked.

"Guess I'll make you a little present, doll, seeing as how we're going to be friends.''

"How nice!'' Melanie arranged her skirt modestly and stretched out on the couch. It really was very comfortable. Mick gave her a fresh set of smog filters and moved the plastic palm tree to shade her from the hazy afternoon sun. Then he settled himself at a workbench nearby while she eagerly turned the pages of the first *True Story*.

Once in a while she looked up and saw him wielding pliers and a small acetylene torch. How lucky she was to have been rescued by him! Of course, fate had been cruel really, matching her with a man who was so nearly right, but twenty years too old for her and not so clean-cut as she would have wished. Still, it was a sign that not all of human existence had to be marred with misery and pain.

After half an hour he put down a soldering iron and handed her the thing he had made. It was a length of silver chain from which hung small items of special meaning in his life. A Hurst gearshift knob, the channel selector from an RCA ColorTune TV, a locket containing a picture of the Big Bopper, the ignition key from a '53 Studebaker, the tremolo arm from a Stratocaster guitar, a GE vacuum tube. Each item had been wired to the slender chain with consummate skill. She turned the assemblage over in her hands and looked at it in wonder. "What is it?" she asked.

"Hey, doll, it's a necklace. Ain't you going to put it on?"

"Oh. Of course.'' She fastened the chain around her neck and arranged the dangling components like the rays of a scrap-metal sun. She hoped there was no oil or grease that might stain her pink cardigan.

"Looks great!'' he exclaimed. "Hey, I gotta take your picture. Wait right there.'' He strode quickly into his apartment, and she heard distant crunching and crashing noises as he searched for a camera amid the piles of salvaged memorabilia.

A shadow passed over the sun. Melanie looked up, hoping it wasn't going to rain. But there were no clouds, just a fluttering shape wheeling around in the sky. She shielded her eyes. Why, it was like a huge bird, or maybe one of those airplanes she remembered from when she was a child. It circled, a black silhouette against the glare. It seemed to be growing larger. She realized with a shock that whatever it was, it was descending directly toward her. "Mick!" she called, sitting up quickly on the couch. "Mick, there's . . . there's something out here!"

7. UNAUTHORIZED ACCESS

"Excuse me, sir, there is an important message."

The Chief Programmer had been idly amusing himself scanning the latest Third World famine figures as the flier slowly descended through the poisonous vapors toward the landing field at the edge of the dome. Roused from his reverie by the neutral voice of the onboard computer, he sighed, removed his free hand from Charlotte's synthetic flesh, and pressed the accept button. "Yes?"

The screen lit up with the face of New York City's police commissioner. "Sir, I have extremely bad news." He coughed, and his eyes shifted nervously. "As yet I do not have a complete report, but I understand that the . . . the Bertha robot has escaped from its escort."

The Chief Programmer waited without speaking. His expression gave no clue to his thoughts.

"I—I didn't want to bother you, sir, but you did emphasize the importance of this assignment, so even though it is not yet clear whether—"

"Who is responsible?" The Chief Programmer stared steadily into the video lens, his face still an expressionless mask.

"I put my top man on it, sir, just as you requested. Chief of Police Henry Jackson. Unfortunately, he injured himself pursuing the robot and is now hospitalized—"

"You put the chief of police on an escort detail? Commissioner, when I told you to use your *top man*, I was not necessarily referring to seniority of rank."

"You weren't?" Breen looked confused.

The Chief Programmer flexed his fingers. He cracked his knuckles. He picked up a digitizer stylus from the computer console and suddenly stabbed its pointed tip savagely into the soft armrest of the pilot's seat. "Send me a picture and job profile of Jackson." The momentary spasm of anger left him as suddenly as it had come.

"Right away, sir." Breen did something with a control panel outside the picturefone's field of view. His hands seemed to be shaking.

The Chief Programmer glanced over his shoulder at the door between the cockpit and the cabin. It was still closed, and he heard no sound of Sullivan stirring back there. "Did you track the robot, as I instructed?" he asked Breen quietly.

The administrator looked even more unhappy. "We did get a trace leading across the East River, but since then the radio beacon implanted in the robot's, ah, earlobe has unaccountably stopped working."

"*Across* the river? Was the robot on a boat?"

"Witnesses at the scene claim he—it—started to fly, sir, with the aid of a gadget it built itself."

The Chief Programmer clenched his jaw and closed his eyes. He made a strange suppressed sound.

"Tired, hon?" Charlotte inquired helpfully. "Hey, why don't I make you a piña colada!"

He waved her silent. "I will obtain satellite tracking

records," he told the cowed, twitching figure on the screen in front of him. "They may possibly show a trace. I will arrange liaison between your police force"—he spoke without bothering to conceal his sneer—"and appropriate federal agencies. You understand?" He punched codes on a console as he spoke.

"Yes, sir. I can guarantee our department's fullest cooperation, sir."

"And in the meantime," the Chief Programmer continued, "if your department finds any trace of the robot, contact me immediately. Do *not* attempt to apprehend it yourselves."

Breen nodded vigorously. "Absolutely, sir."

"Perhaps you would repeat what I just said so we can be sure there is no misunderstanding this time." The Chief Programmer give a thin smile.

"If my men, ah, find evidence of the location of the robot, I will contact you, and will not attempt to arrest . . . ah, apprehend . . . the suspect."

The smile widened fractionally. "Very good, Commissioner. Well done."

"Thank you, sir. Er, I have the file on Jackson. Shall I display it?"

"Yes."

"Thank you, sir. Have a nice day, sir." The screen blanked, then lit up with a full-face picture of Jackson taken twenty years ago. As the flier gradually sank toward its landing field under autopilot control, the Chief Programmer studied Jackson's face, then scrolled through the man's history of bureaucratic gamesmanship and red-tape manipulation. There was something oddly familiar about him. As Jackson's earliest job assignments appeared on the screen, suddenly the Chief Programmer sat straight up in his chair. "Patrolman in Central Park!" he exclaimed.

"Are you feeling all right, hon?" Charlotte looked at him with baffled concern. She lacked the programming or the experience to know how to react to such unprecedented outbursts of emotion from her mentor.

"I have never felt better," he said slowly. His hand

absentmindedly strayed under her miniskirt and massaged
her left buttock while he studied Jackson's face. He remembered it all, now. Back in the early sixties, he'd been fresh
out of college, on the night shift at IBM. He'd walked
home through the park. He remembered Jackson getting
out of a patrol car on the perimeter road and ambling over,
smacking his billy club into his hand. Jackson grinning at
him, saying, "Past your bedtime, nigger." Jackson swing-
ing his club, his fists; Jackson kicking him as he lay
groaning on the ground, then laughing and driving away.

The Chief Programmer's hand clenched suddenly, making Charlotte squeal with surprise and confusion. At last,
after all these years . . .

The flier hovered, waiting for him to disconnect the
autopilot and engage manual control for the last few feet of
the descent. He ignored it and punched complex codes
onto his personal terminal linked directly to Computer
Central. Using privileged passwords for access, he quickly
networked his way through to the New York City hospital
system. He fed in Jackson's Social Security number, then
sighed with quiet satisfaction when he saw the response.
Jackson was at Bellevue Hospital, undergoing treatment
for concussion and a possible fractured skull.

The Chief Programmer stared out at nothing in particular, with colorless eyes. He flexed his fingers like a con-
cert pianist about to begin a virtuoso performance. Swiftly,
without bothering to check the display screen, he began
feeding new command codes to the hospital computers.

8. MISSION OF MERCY

He fell from the sky like an angel and landed lightly at Melanie's feet. "Please do not be alarmed," he told her.

She stared at him with wide eyes. "Who are you?" she blurted, clutching the romance magazine between her hands as if it would serve as some kind of shield.

He seemed not to have heard her. He looked around at the heaps of salvaged equipment littering the patio. "More hardware," he mused. "I saw it from the sky." His attention shifted to her necklace. He stepped tentatively closer, beside the G-couch. He reached to touch the dangling components. "May I?"

Melanie flinched back. But there was a diffidence, a gentleness about him that made her feel mesmerized. He touched the icons wired to the silver chain and smiled happily. Then he saw the magazine that Melanie was holding. "May I look at this?"

"Sure!" Her voice sounded scared and much too loud. She pushed the magazine quickly into his hands. "Mick!" she shouted. "Mick, come out here!"

The man in the robe studied the magazine cover. "They are like us," he said, pointing at the picture of a handsome surgeon and a cute young nurse staring romantically into each other's eyes. Melanie looked, and saw he was right: she did resemble the nurse, and he was every bit as handsome as the doctor.

"But who are you?" she asked again. "How did you

fly like that? Do you work for the government or something? Are you a scientist?''

He frowned. "It is hard for me to remember anything."

"You have amnesia! Wow!" She thought of all the stories she had read in which the hero had lost his memory. He always turned out to be someone really important. "Mick!" she called. "Mick, you have to come out here! Hurry!"

He was, in fact, just emerging from his living room, holding an old Polaroid camera. He saw the man in white, and stopped short. "Hey," he said, "what gives?" He put the camera aside and reached for his switchblade.

"I think he's harmless," said Melanie, scrambling off the couch and running to Mick's side. She took his arm. The heavy black leather smelled of oil and grease and seemed reassuring under her hands.

"Yes, I am harmless," the man in white agreed.

"You talk funny," said Mick. He fingered his switchblade, but made no move to open it. "What's that on your chest?"

"Antigravity. It lifts me." He frowned. "I am so confused, I am not sure how I made it."

Mick laughed. "Antigravity, huh? Now that's something I'd like to see."

"Of course, if you wish." He obligingly fiddled with the mess of wire and string. The neon bulb lit up. The string tightened. His feet lifted a few inches. "The clock battery is not powerful," he explained apologetically. "It was all that was available."

Mick stared stupidly. He walked around behind the man, then dropped down on his hands and knees and peered at the gap between his feet and the floor. Finally he stood up and peered at the assemblage of wires stuffed in the back of the digital clock. "Can I see that? I got to see that."

The man in white made an adjustment, and his feet settled back down onto the floor. He undid the harness of nylon string and handed the whole thing to Mick. "We can build many more interesting things with your hardware here," he said.

"We can, huh?" Mick turned the clock, wire, and string over in his hands. "You some kind of egghead genius, or what?"

"He's lost his memory," Melanie explained. She looked up at him. "Can you remember your name?"

"They were calling me Bertha," he said slowly.

Melanie shook her head. "That's a girl's name. You must have it wrong. Let's call you 'Burt' till we find out for sure."

He smiled and nodded happily. "Burt. All right."

She touched his white gown. "And we have to get you some respectable clothes. Were you in a hospital?"

He frowned. "For a long time. There were painful tests, with electricity."

"Oh my goodness! That's terrible!" Melanie reached out and took his hand. There was something about him that made her feel a strange yearning. A quality of inno-cence. He seemed somehow *sinless,* she realized, as if he had never been touched by all the greed and hate in the world. "Would you like something to eat?"

"Oh yes, I am hungry."

"Sit down, sit down on the couch. Mick, he needs food and clothes."

"I got to figure how this screwball gadget works." He peered in the opened back of the digital clock.

She quickly plucked it out of his hands. "There's time for that later. This man needs our help, Mick." There was a look in her eyes that allowed no room for argument.

"So what's the first thing you remember?" Melanie asked as the man in white eagerly consumed a State Food ration pack and a mug of coffee substitute, while Mick went in search of some suitable clothes.

"I opened my eyes and I was in a white room," he said slowly. "There were many people looking at me. Scien-tists. They were very excited. Then, when it became appar-ent that I did not know how to talk, they became unhappy."

"You forgot how to speak!"

"Possibly I never knew. But I was able to learn quickly, although I notice I do not talk as fluently as you, Melanie."

She blushed prettily, and patted his hand. "You talk just fine. You must have been in a terrible accident."

"An accident. Perhaps there was an accident. The scientists think something went wrong while I was in the tank."

Her eyes widened. "A tank? You were in the army!"

"Perhaps I have not been clear. You see, I am indistinguishable from a human being, except for one thing." He stood up and started unbuttoning his robe.

"Oh no, please don't show me your scars! Maybe— maybe later, if we get to know each other better."

"Hey, dig this set of threads, daddy-o," said Mick, walking onto the patio with a pair of pink peg slacks, matching pink socks, pointed-toed shoes with Cuban heels, a black rayon shirt, and a narrow white knit tie. "Cool, huh?"

"Mick, do you have anything less, you know, in the groove?" Melanie interrupted as the man in white turned the clothes over in his hands and frowned, holding them first one way up, then the other.

"Well, I guess," Mick said dubiously.

"Why don't you two guys go pick out something nice while I do the dishes?" she suggested.

A little later, Burt was fitted out in narrow corduroy pants, loafers, a shirt with a button-down collar, and a jacket with wide padded shoulders. He looked like a young college grad who had just stepped out of a time machine from fifty years ago. "Neat-o!" Melanie exclaimed, clapping her hands.

"I am pleased to make you happy," he said politely.

"So let's build something," said Mick. He gestured to his workbench. "What else can you do? Matter transmission? Telepathy? Transmutation of metals? Super-weapons?"

Melanie put her hands on her hips. "Mick! He's recovering from a *serious accident!*"

Burt was frowning. "But I would like to be of help,"

he said. He walked over to the workbench and started fingering various components: circuit boards, capacitors, ICs, pieces of cardboard, empty ration packs. "It is so hard to remember."

"You think you were in a research lab?" said Mick. "With computers and that kind of jazz? Was that where you learned this stuff?"

"Yes, that is right." He fiddled aimlessly with some components. "A big computer taught me everything that I know."

Mick nodded to himself. "I always knew the government was keeping things secret from the public."

Burt looked up. "Secret. Yes, that is right, there were many secrets which I was programmed not to reveal. They were important. I wish I could—"

"Don't overexert yourself," Melanie told him. She patted him gently on the arm. "Maybe you should go for a little walk, to try to relax and take your mind off things."

"Oh yes, I would like that!" He dropped the components.

Mick opened his mouth to protest, but Melanie gave him a warning look. "Maybe we should go to the entertainment center," Melanie went on. "That sounded like a nice place."

The three of them walked along a cracked concrete path matted with weeds, the sluggish river on one side, derelict condos on the other, cubist architecture half buried under ivy and kudzu vines.

"See the wires there?" Mick pointed to cables dangling from a rusty latticework tower. "Used to be a little car that ran on them wires, in and out of Manhattan. That's how commuters went to work. But there wasn't nothing to do here on the island, nothing shaking but the leaves on the trees. So they built Fun City." He pointed to a big concrete building topped with neon signs that were dead, bent silhouettes against the sky. "State-of-the-art entertainment. Like a cybernetic mall."

"What's a mall?" Melanie asked.

Mick sighed. "Before your time, doll. It don't matter

now. Kids used to hang out there; like at—at drive-in hamburger stands."

"Oh, now I understand."

Burt had wandered to the edge of the river and was staring at the peasant people plying the river with their fishing nets. "They are looking for food?"

Mick nodded. "Yep. State rations only go so far."

"If there were fewer people," Burt said thoughtfully, "there would be more food for each person."

"The peps don't see it that way. They figure, the more of them there are, the more clout they got. And they're right; that's how they muscled in on this town."

"People are very complicated," said Burt. "Machines are simpler."

"That may be so," said Melanie. "But machines can't feel and hope and cry and fall in love."

Burt turned and stared at her strangely. He touched her shoulder, then the necklace of mechanical components that she was still wearing. "I would like you to teach me about these things such as hope and love," he said.

Melanie felt her cheeks turning red. "I—I'll try," she blurted.

Mick looked from one of them to the other and grinned. He started whistling "Could This Be Magic?"

"You stop that!" Melanie scolded him.

Mick led the way into what had once been a plush lobby. The red carpet was covered in mold and mildew, exotic rainbow-patterned wallpaper was dangling in dilapidated strips, and huge mirrors lay in fragments on the floor. "I didn't fix none of this," Mick explained, "so's not to attract attention." He vaulted the turnstiles, went to a door at the back, unlocked it, and did something inside a metal panel. Some of the lobby lights came to life. "Let's take the elevator," he said.

"A real elevator!" Melanie clapped her hands with delight as the pair of stainless steel doors slid open. She walked in and started eagerly pressing buttons. "I used to go for rides in the elevators at the Chrysler Building when

I was a kid. It was a whole lot of fun.'' Her expression clouded for a moment as she remembered those days of childhood innocence, forever lost.

"We'll start on the second floor," Mick said. "I got some of the effects working there."

The elevator took the three of them up, then opened its doors onto a corridor whose walls shimmered in a 3-D imitation of a verdant forest. "This here is what they used to call Electronic Eden," Mick explained. A scratchy tape of birdsong was playing, and a fake breeze wafted down the hallway, smelling faintly of Lysol. A giant mechanical rabbit hopped toward them, its ears flopping, tail bobbing, limbs squeaking. "Hello Mick!" it said in a cute but scratchy electronic voice.

"This is Ronald Rabbit," said Mick. He patted the creature's head, where patches of fake fur had fallen out and dented aluminum was showing through. "Ronald, this is my friend Melanie, and this is, uh, Burt. Say hi to them."

Ronald Rabbit turned obediently toward Melanie. "Hello Mick!" he squawked. He turned to Burt. "Hello Mick!" he squawked again. He attempted to turn around, but fell on his side. His legs twitched. "Help!" he exclaimed.

Mick pulled him back upright.

"Hey, let's go for a walk!" said Ronald Rabbit.

They followed him along the corridor, into a room done up as a woodland glade. Fake trees and bushes were scattered across a floor that sank underfoot like soft moss. Plastic foliage dangled from a tangle of branches that hid most of the ceiling. Mechanical birds were chirping. A giant mouse came hobbling over, its motors whining. It was followed by a lurching, clucking, three-foot-tall chicken.

"These are my other two pals," said Mick. "This one's Mister Mouse, and here's Cheerful Chicken."

"I just laid an egg!" said Mister Mouse.

"Mick, did you spend a lot of time alone here?" Melanie asked, giving him a worried, searching look.

"Well, you know, it was something to do."

"Why was this room built?" Burt asked.

"I want some cheese!" interrupted Cheerful Chicken.

"Later," Mick told him. He turned to Burt. "They built this place so kids could get into the grass and trees and stuff, on account of there wasn't none of the real thing left. Not within twenty miles, anyhow. Guys used to come here and make out with girls." He gestured at little scenic hollows in the mossy pseudo-turf.

"Make out?" Burt looked puzzled.

"You know, kissing and cuddling and like that. You should ask Melanie about it sometime."

"Mick!" She stamped her foot. "How dare you!"

"You do not wish to tell me, Melanie?" said Burt.

"This isn't the right time to talk about that kind of thing," she answered demurely.

"Here comes Joe!" Ronald Rabbit put in.

A ragged human figure was picking his way between the trees, stepping through golden shafts of electric sunshine striking down through the canopy of fake foliage above. He was a stooped old man dressed in rags. His head was bald. A white beard hung almost to his waist. "Mick?" he called. "That you, Mick?"

"Yeah, Joe. What's shaking? I want you to meet Melanie, here, and Burt, two friends of mine."

The old man stopped and peered dubiously from one to the next. " 'Scuse me if I don't shake hands," he muttered. "The arthritis is bad. Very painful." He turned to Mick. "You got any food with you?"

"I brought you a load just a couple days back," Mick protested.

Burt was deep in thought. "Arthritis," he said suddenly, "is a painful inflammation of joint structures leading to stiffness, pain, and ultimately total disability and invalidism!"

The old man turned and glared at him. "You think that's funny, son, you ought to try it."

"No, it is not funny," said Burt. "I am having trouble remembering things. It just came into my head. But arthritis should be an easy thing to cure."

"Who is this nut?" Joe the hobo complained to Mick.

"He's got amnesia," said Mick. "But he used to be a scientist."

"I would like to help you, Mr. Joe, and if there are other people here, I would help them too," Burt offered. "I think there is hardware at Mick's home that would build a simple machine to restore the tissues damaged by arthritis, and other degenerative diseases also."

"How wonderful!" Melanie exclaimed.

"There's guys upstairs suffering from every disease in the book," said the old hobo. "You want to look at 'em?"

"Oh yes. Please."

"Well, I s'pose it can't do no harm." He led the way through the woodland landscape toward a distant Emergency Exit sign.

Ronald Rabbit stood beside Cheerful Chicken and Mister Mouse. He watched the humans leave. "Hello, Mick?" he said hopefully.

The emergency stairwell was cold and dark and dank. "We could've taken the elevator," Melanie complained.

"Don't trust them things," said Hobo Joe. He pulled open a heavy metal door on the second floor. "Watch how you walk in here."

"Joe and the other old guys live in the upside-down-and-sideways rooms," said Mick. "Says they got used to it, and now they couldn't live anyplace else."

The place was furnished like a large, opulent living room, except that all the furniture, including overstuffed armchairs, an oriental rug, and a large dining table set for dinner, was mounted on one of the walls. A chandelier protruded stiffly from the opposite wall, and on the real ceiling, oil paintings hung either side of a huge marble fireplace. To disturb the senses still further, the whole room was canted at an angle.

Two hairy old men were sitting in armchairs that they had removed from the display and placed in one corner, beside stacks of State Food ration packs and a heap of old blankets. They were passing a plastipac of wine to and fro.

"Hey, honey," one of the oldsters exclaimed, seeing Melanie, "come on over and have a drink, why doncha?"

"I'd wash her windshield anytime," said his companion. He clutched his stomach and wheezed with laughter, exposing three teeth.

Burt strode over to him, ignoring the disorienting decor. "You seem to be suffering from halitosis, cirrhosis of the liver, fallen arches, sciatica, duodenal ulcers, and prostatitis," he said after a quick examination.

The old man turned to his companion. "Looks like Mick's brought us his personal physician!" He chuckled some more.

"You also need dental work," said Burt. "I'm not sure that I can deal with all of these problems."

"Hey, doc," called the other old man. "You got anything for a case of hemorrhoids? I mean it, doc. They're driving me bananas."

"Yes, that can be cured," said Burt after a moment's thought. He turned to Mick. "We must go back to your home and assemble some devices."

Mick laughed uneasily. "You mean it, don't you?"

Burt nodded. "Of course." He turned suddenly to Melanie. "Will you help me?"

She looked into his eyes and felt a tightness in her throat. She remembered the picture on the cover of the romance magazine: the handsome doctor, the beautiful young nurse. She nodded eagerly. "I'll do whatever you say."

As afternoon faded into evening, many miracle cures were accomplished in Fun City. Burt's homemade equipment was primitive, lashed together with everyday items such as flashlight batteries, spectacle lenses, electromagnets, and a tokamak he found lying around in Mick's basement. But it worked, and soon he was eradicating ailments ranging from athlete's foot to intestinal polyps.

"I don't get it," Mick said as yet another oldster emerged from the healing rays projected from the guts of a rewired CB radio and proclaimed that his arthritis had been banished. "If you know how to do all this, someone told you, right?"

"That is a logical deduction," Burt agreed.

"So how come no one's getting rich selling these techniques? How come the government's keeping 'em locked up?"

"That I do not know," said Burt, applying electrodes to a hobo's stomach and subjecting it to a brief low-voltage pulse while bombarding it with ultrasound from a heavily modified videodisc player. "Your ulcer should bother you no further," he said to the old man, "although I would suggest taking antacid tablets if you intend to continue drinking alcohol."

"Mick, you know perfectly well that Burt has lost his memory," Melanie chided him. "He can't be expected to know all the answers."

"It is true. I make these things"—Burt gestured at the components—"by intuition. I cannot explain it. I wish I could." He looked away into space for a moment. "You know, I believe I could do even more if we could get real medical equipment for me to modify. And perhaps I could find drugs to help my memory, also."

Melanie turned to Mick. "Do you know a place where they throw out old medical gadgets? Or somewhere that sells them cheaply?"

He shook his head. "Never seen none. But I figure it shouldn't be too tough. We can make it across the river just before it gets light, go in and take whatever we need."

Melanie hated to hear him talk so casually about stealing things, even if it was for a good cause. "What is this place?" she asked.

"Bellevue, of course. Biggest hospital in the state."

That night, the oldsters threw a celebration party. There was a lot of drinking and dancing. Melanie showed Burt how to do the Twist, the Dog, the Madison, and the Pony, and when he got tired and had to sit down, she taught him the Hand-Jive. "No one ever wanted to dance with me at the Chrysler Building," she told him. "This is just wonderful!"

"It is fun," he agreed. "You are a good person, Melanie." He patted her hand. "But I think I would like to take a walk," he said. "I need to see the nighttime."

"Why, of course!"

Moments later, they were strolling beside the river. On the opposite shore stood the eroded towers of Manhattan. "Aren't the lights lovely?" said Melanie. "Why, there must be a candle in every window." She took Burt's hand.

He looked up from the city to the night sky. "Those are stars," he said, picking out the occasional bright pinpoint that showed through the smog. "I do not think I have ever seen stars before. They are large bodies of incandescent gas, many millions of miles away."

Melanie tugged at his hand.

He looked from the sky to her face. "What is it, Melanie?"

She stood in front of him, staring into his eyes. She ran the palms of her hands up his chest, and then slowly linked her hands behind his neck. Her pulse beat fast as she moved closer till her body was just touching his.

"There is something you want?" He seemed puzzled.

"Isn't there something *you* want? Or—" She hesitated, shocked by her own boldness but driven by her aching need for him. "Or have you forgotten how to give a girl a kiss?"

"Oh." He smiled. "A kiss? Maybe you will have to show me."

He touched his lips to hers. She felt her strength ebb. She fell against him and clung to him. The kiss seemed to last forever.

Melanie finally pulled free when she realized she was losing her self-control. She didn't want him to think she was too easy. She tried to remember what you were supposed to say at times like this, on your first date.

"It is late," he said, before she could put the words together in her head.

"Gee, I guess it is," she agreed. "But you still respect me, don't you? I mean—"

He smiled at her. "I think we should go to bed. Do you concur?"

She stepped back in sudden shock. "You don't mean . . . with each other?"

He frowned. "Of course not. That is what married people do; and, Melanie, I hardly know you."

She gave a little sigh of relief. He wasn't like Crosby and all the others. For the first time, she dared to let herself think: Could this be love?

9. DESTINATION: DESTINY

Lennon paced the tiled floor of what had once been the Cloud Club, high in the spire of the Chrysler Building. Exotic vegetation loomed around him, shadowy forms barely visible in the smog-yellow moonlight: cannabis sativa, peyote cacti, yage, belladonna, coca plants, painstakingly cultivated by members of the commune. He chewed idly on an ibogaine root, then threw it aside, walked to a window, and stared broodingly at the urban panorama. Somewhere, he knew, Melanie was out there.

Lennon heard footsteps wearily climbing the emergency stairs. He turned and saw an emaciated, hairy figure shuffling in, lighting his way with a tallow candle. "Hey, Crosby," he called softly. "What's happening, man?"

"Your old lady said as how you were up here," said Crosby.

"Which one?"

Crosby scratched his head. "Janis, I think. Hey, you want a toke?" He held out a half-smoked joint.

"No thanks. Getting high doesn't do it for me right now."

"That's a bummer." Crosby relit the joint with his sputtering candle, and inhaled deeply.

"I shouldn't have laid it on her like that," said Lennon.

Crosby didn't answer.

"I shouldn't have told Melanie to split, man."

Crosby remained silent.

"I always say, do your own thing, but I'm not cool enough to let my own kid do hers."

Crosby let out his lungful of smoke. He gasped, took a deep breath, coughed, and belched.

"What am I going to do, man?" Lennon went on. "She could be in deep shit out there."

"Have you checked your chart?"

"No, but you're right, I should do that. You think Ursula has crashed yet?"

"Hell, it's only four, she'll be around. Let's go."

They descended a dozen flights of stairs and found their way along a shadowy corridor. The building seemed strangely silent. After three A.M., the Muzak system shut down: everyone was too busy getting high to bother pedaling the electric generator. Up ahead, however, came sounds of Mistress Ursula playing acoustic guitar and softly singing "California Dreamin'."

"Peace," said Lennon, ducking around the tapestry hanging in the doorway.

"Why, Lennon, my love." She put her guitar aside and beamed at him. She was a little old lady with pink cheeks and curly gray hair. Rumor had it she was pushing eighty, which violated the dictum, *Never trust anyone over sixty-five*. Still, as herbalist, chief astrologer, and white-magic witch, she had a special status in the commune.

She turned to Crosby as he followed Lennon into the cubicle. "And how are you, dear?" She gave him a slightly vexed look. "Have you gone off your macrobiotic diet again? Too much yin, by the look of you."

"Well, you know." He avoided her eyes.

"I made some fresh rice balls just yesterday," she told him. "I think you should have one right now, don't you?"

"Uh, okay." He pulled out a pair of chopsticks from the pocket of his caftan.

"I don't want to hassle you, Ursula," said Lennon, scratching his beard, "but I was wondering . . ."

She peeled seaweed off a rice ball, dumped it into a wooden bowl, and handed it to Crosby. "You want me to cast your horoscope," she said.

"Well, yes." Lennon lowered his bulk onto a small wooden stool beneath a Peter Max poster of cherubs walking hand-in-hand through a wheat field. "See, I been thinking maybe I should go out looking for Melanie, but first—"

"Quite right." She pulled out a huge vinyl-bound ledger that dated back to the days when this section of the Chrysler Building had been occupied by the accounting department of the Acme Stamped-Metal Buckle and Fastener Co. Pages of credits and debits had long since been ripped out, the rest of the volume crammed full of astrological charts, notes on graphology, macrobiotic recipes, herbal remedies, reflexology, and homeopathic formulae, all written in Ursula's cramped, angular hand.

"Make yourself comfortable, my sweet," she told Lennon with what was intended as an intimate smile. "This may take a few minutes."

In fact, it took most of the next hour. She checked the planetary ephemera, referred to Lennon's personal chart, factored in his element, his exaltation, his blood group, and his birthstone, and paused to make herself some herbal tea before rendering her final verdict. The advice was complicated, Saturn currently being in the seventh house, Mars being in opposition to Venus, Leo being Lennon's sun sign, and the Moon currently being in Scorpio. "What it comes down to, though," she finished up, "is that anytime in the next week, if you go outside something bad will probably happen to you; and even if it doesn't, you're unlikely to find her anyway."

"That's a drag," said Lennon.

"However"—she turned to Crosby, who had finished his rice and was slumped against one wall meditatively picking pieces of dry skin from between his toes—"I seem to remember, Crosby, your chart would make you much better aligned with the zodiac right now. Just let me check."

Another half-hour later, the verdict was clear: Crosby was optimally placed, in the web of cosmic forces, to locate Lennon's missing daughter.

"You're sure about that?" he asked dubiously.

"Well, let's see, how many letters are in your name?" He frowned. "Well, six."

"And your letters add up to eighty-two, which sums to ten, which sums to one, the unity! And Melanie's name contains seven letters, which sum to sixty, which sums to six. Let me just check." She consulted her book. "You and she have a compatibility of .934. Really, that is quite amazing."

"Compatibility?" said Crosby. "Forget it. I never did get to ball that chick."

"Precisely because you and she were so similar," Ursula explained with patient condescension. "Numerologically compatible people often rebel against each other. They're like twins who fight all the time."

"Oh." Crosby scratched his head. "But suppose I went out there. How would I know where to look?"

"We must cast the I-Ching." She pulled out a little handmade leather pouch, from which she took three antique subway tokens. "You throw it, Crosby."

She drew his hexagram in the big ledger as the coins fell six times on the rush matting of the cubicle floor. "Number twenty-eight!" she exclaimed. "That which the seeker values least is soonest lost. At a time of uncertainty, wealth lies across the great water. There is no blame."

"I don't get it," said Lennon after a moment's silence.

"It's obvious." She closed the book. "You're not to blame for her leaving home."

"But it could mean *she's* not to blame."

"She wasn't the one who cast the I-Ching, dear."

"Neither was I. Crosby did."

"But she's your daughter, isn't she? Now, what do you value most?"

Lennon thought hard. "Melanie. That's why I'm so uptight."

"No, dear. You valued her least. That's why you let her leave, and now *that which the seeker values least is soonest lost*. Understand?"

"Oh." Lennon nodded. "Uh-huh. I get it."

"Now, *wealth lies across the great water*. That's clear enough."

Lennon and Crosby looked at each other. "I hear things ain't so tough in Australia right now," Crosby suggested.

"No, no! Not material wealth, spiritual wealth! It refers to Melanie. She has clearly traveled over some water."

"She's split for New Jersey!" Crosby exclaimed. "Hey, far out!"

Ursula nodded happily. "First thing tomorrow," she told him, "as soon as you wake up—before noon, if possible—you must go out in search of her. The quest may at times be arduous . . ."

"Uh," muttered Crosby.

". . . but if you pause often, close your eyes, visualize Melanie's face clearly, and follow your instincts, I have no doubt you will find her. I'll make up a backpack for you to take, with rice cakes and bean paste; and here is a lucky rat's foot that you should carry at all times." She handed him a withered little furry paw on a chain. "Put it on, dear."

"Oh. Must I?"

"Now you'll need to get some rest."

Crosby stood up. Lennon also got to his feet. He wrapped his arms around Crosby. "Hey, you're a true brother."

"Forget it, man, it's nothing." With his face pressed into Lennon's satin sari, his voice was barely audible.

"You know I'd go myself," said Lennon, "if it wasn't for the planets and that."

"Sure, I can dig it. Hey, I better go crash, man."

Lennon pounded Crosby on the back. "Stay cool."

"Absolutely." Crosby extracted himself from the bear hug.

"Remember, close your eyes and think of her, anytime you feel in doubt," Ursula told him.

"Yeah. Yeah, I'll do that." He relit his tallow candle from the kerosene heater and shuffled out.

"Makes me feel good to know where she's at," said Lennon. "I owe you one, Ursula."

She set aside her book and tugged her granny dress up and over her withered skin. "Think nothing of it." She patted the futon beside her. "Just you come here and make yourself comfortable."

10. MAN OF PARTS

"Help!" screamed Henry Jackson. He had woken up five minutes ago to find himself strapped to a bed in a cubicle the size of a small elevator. His head throbbed. He was dizzy and delirious.

A glaring, blaring thirty-inch color TV was suspended in front of his face so close that he could almost touch the screen with his nose. "Okay, Marcia," a game show host was saying, his arm around the shoulders of a jittery, malnourished woman grinning dumbly into the camera. "It's *crackpot jackpot time!* And here's what you can win! How's about a *Homeglo room heater?* Burns anything— newspapers, old books, even domestic garbage! Your living cubicle need never be cold again! From Homeglo, today's experts in environmental comfort! But that's not all!"

"Doctor! Nurse!" Jackson screamed. "What the hell is going on here?"

"—a genuine polyester raincoat and matching *real leather shoes!*"

Jackson yanked futilely at the restraints. They gripped his arms, chest, hips, and both legs. "Goddamn it!"

"But that's still not all," the TV host was saying with a big grin. "We have something extra: this *beautiful tandem pedmobile!* With inflatable tires, a certified cast-iron frame, three-speed gear change, and a *weatherproof roof of recycled cotton!*" The audience screamed with hysteria and the contestant buried her face in her hands and sobbed uncontrollably. "Just answer this simple question," the host was saying. "You have ten seconds, Marcia, to tell me: Who discovered the United States of America?"

Jackson closed his eyes and whimpered and banged his head against his pillow.

The television screen suddenly went dark, and its blaring loudspeaker died, leaving a ringing in Jackson's ears. Then the screen lit up with a man's face, gray-haired, studious, frowning with friendly concern. "Well, good morning to you, Mr. Jackson," the face said in mellow, resonant tones. "You seem to be feeling better already."

Jackson panted for breath, exhausted by his temper tantrum. "Who are you?"

"I'm your doctor, Mr. Jackson. You're in Bellevue Hospital, and you're doing just fine."

Jackson glowered up at the screen. "Why the hell am I strapped to the bed like this?"

"You were admitted suffering concussion, with a possible fractured skull. I understand you hit your head on a fire hydrant." The face on the screen gave a wry smile, as if Jackson's injuries were such a thing of the past, they were now no more than a matter of nostalgic amusement. "Well, no fracture showed up on the X rays, and we fixed the concussion with some of those new wonder drugs you've been hearing about."

"I said, Why am I strapped to the bed?" Jackson interrupted. "And if I'm in such good shape, how about letting me out of here?'' He remembered the trillion-dollar robot drifting out of his reach, into the sky. He twisted and yanked at the restraining straps.

''Unfortunately,'' the face on the screen continued smoothly, ''while performing a routine checkup, we found a few other things that needed attention. Since you have gold-rated medical coverage as a city employee, we went ahead and fixed them.''

''Fixed what?'' Jackson stopped struggling abruptly.

''Just a few routine replacements. Let's see, you have a prosthetic leg, artificial kidneys, plastiflex left hand, and an artificial left eye.''

''What!'' Jackson tried to move his legs. One of them jerked strangely. He clenched his left fist. There was a whining of tiny motors, and a metallic clicking noise. He shut his right eye. Through his left, colors had a strange blue tinge, and the TV picture was hopelessly blurred.

''When you consider that you've only been in the hospital just over twelve hours, I think you'll agree modern medicine has done a pretty impressive job,'' the face on the screen finished up.

''I'll sue!'' Jackson yelled. ''Did you do this? Were you the surgeon?'' He writhed helplessly. ''I'll have you arrested. Damn it, I'll arrest you myself! You're under arrest right now, fella! I'm Chief of Police, do you understand that? Jesus H. Christ!''

''We're sorry to inconvenience you, Mr. Jackson,'' the face continued, ''but we have to get the results of one last set of tests before we can discharge you from our care. You know, here at Bellevue, we take our responsibilities pretty seriously.'' He chuckled. ''And most of our patients wouldn't have it any other way. Now, while you're waiting, how about some Valium? Or perhaps you'd like to watch some more television?''

''No!'' Jackson screamed.

Who had done this to him? It had to be part of the same conspiracy. Breen? His wife? One of his subordinates? By God, he'd make them pay! And this doctor, whoever he was, he'd have him disbarred. He squinted at the man's face. "Wait a minute. Wait a goddamned minute! You're not a man at all!"

The man's face nodded agreeably. "Bellevue leads the Free World in hospital automation, Mr. Jackson. The image you are watching is generated from a videodisc, animated by a natural-language processor. Almost all the medical procedures here are conducted by industrial robots. Everything is supervised by expert systems possessing the combined medical experience of more than three thousand of America's most highly qualified physicians. As a result, malpractice and human error have been completely eliminated. For those with gold-rated medical credit, Mr. Jackson, this truly is tomorrow's health care available today!"

Jackson tried to get a grip on himself. There was no point in screaming at a nonperson. "Listen, you," he said, slowly and distinctly, "I want to talk to a human being. A hospital administrator, if possible. And I want it *now*."

"I'm afraid that won't be possible," the face replied. "The time is six-eleven A.M., and none of the human staff arrives before nine. I will, however, file a copy of your request."

"Look," said Jackson, "I have to get out of here. I am in the middle of an important assignment, do you understand?" Again he remembered the scene on Third Avenue as the trillion-dollar robot escaped into the sky. Suddenly his control cracked. *"Do you understand?"* he screamed, clawing at the sheets.

"One moment." The face vanished and was replaced by a picture of a vase of flowers. Soft music started playing: "The Girl from Ipanema," performed by an orchestra of singing strings.

"Come back!" Jackson shouted. He slumped back onto the bed, overwhelmed by an intense wave of self-pity. He started weeping. Unfair, it was all unfair.

"Henry? Henry, are you there?"

It was his wife's voice. He tried to blink the tears away. Her face had appeared on the screen instead of the vase of flowers, and the music had stopped.

"Henry, are you all right?"

He fought down the waves of misery and despair. If she saw any weakness on his part, she'd only take advantage of it. And if she was the one who had done this to him, he didn't want to allow her a moment's satisfaction. "Just here for a few tests," he muttered, trying to assess her image with his good eye.

"Henry, what *happened?* How could you *do* this? After I begged for you not to go outside. I've been crazy with worry, just out of my mind!"

He tried to decide how much of her act was genuine, and realized he couldn't trust any of it. "Breen told you where I was?" he asked her carefully.

"Yes, yes, he telephoned me."

"Good. Did he say if they'd caught the robot? The thing I was supposed to be keeping in my custody. Have they found it?"

Her face worked with a mixture of emotions. "Is that all you can think about at a time like this, Henry? Your *job?*"

"Just set my mind at rest, dearest." He tried to give her his best ingratiating, obsequious smile. It was an immense effort.

"Well, Mr. Breen didn't say anything about that thing, that robot." She sniffed as if to indicate she was going into these details purely for his benefit, even though it cost her a certain amount of pain. "But I did hear something on the news."

"What, what was that?" He instinctively tried to sit up, and grunted with irritation as the straps held him back.

"First you must tell me when you're coming home, Henry."

"I don't know!" He fought back his anger. "Dearest, they haven't told me. Today, I hope. I'll be there today, okay? Now tell me what they said on the news. It's very important."

"Well, it escaped," she said.

He groaned. "Cynthia, I already *know* that. It's my fault that it escaped."

"And they haven't been able to find it."

"Hah!" Jackson exclaimed.

She drew a deep breath. "Now, Henry, I want you here. Otherwise, I really don't see how I'm supposed to cope."

"If you want me back, you might consider coming down here and getting them to let me out!" he snapped at her.

"You mean, you expect me to go outside?" she stammered.

The fone link cut her off abruptly. The smiling face of the pseudo-doctor reappeared. "Mr. Jackson—can I call you Henry?—I'm sorry to interrupt the call from your wife like this. But we just analyzed those tests I told you about, and I have to tell you we picked up another little problem. Now, I don't want you to worry, because it's really nothing serious."

"What, what is it now?" Jackson blinked, trying to adjust.

"Well, Henry, it's what we doctors call a malignant tumor. Which is a fancy way of saying a little problem with some of your cells, which are growing in a way we don't want them to."

"Cancer, you mean? I've got cancer?"

"Now, really, it's nothing to get excited about. These little cells are all in one place, and with lasers we can snip them out so fast you won't even know it."

"Where? Where are they?"

"As near as we can figure it, Henry, they're growing inside your aorta. That's a fancy technical word for the big pipe that runs into the organ which you refer to as your heart."

"*Heart* cancer? But . . . I've never even heard of it!" He struggled futilely in the straps. "I don't believe it even exists!"

"The condition is rare," the pseudo-doctor agreed, "but I can tell you, Henry, we're well-equipped to deal with it."

Double doors opened automatically in the wall at the foot of Jackson's bed. The TV hinged up out of the way. Sweet music started playing again—"The Tennessee Waltz" this time—louder than before. Jackson's bed jerked under him, then rolled smoothly out of the room into the hospital beyond. He craned his neck and glimpsed a huge space like a factory, filled with machines. There was a smell of formaldehyde. He heard whirring, clattering equipment, an occasional zinging noise like a dentist's drill, and intermittent human screams, almost lost in the melody of a thousand violins.

Jackson's bed started up a ramp that led to something like an assembly line. Mechanical arms were mounted at intervals, tipped with glittering implements. Fierce white lights beamed down.

Jackson jerked and twitched. With a great effort, he managed to slide his left arm halfway up through the straps. Then his new prosthetic hand got caught. But that turned out to be an advantage. He twisted his wrist, and found that the new joint offered much more latitude than the old. He managed to get a grip on the strap with his metal fingers. He wrenched hard, and his sharp new steel fingernails sliced through the webbing.

He glanced anxiously ahead. His bed was approaching the first of the machines, a fearsome thing with multiple arms terminating in stethoscope, tongue depressor, rubber mallet, blood-pressure collar, hypodermic needle, and some other gadgets that looked like a big pair of pliers and a saber saw.

With desperate strength, Jackson twisted and managed to chop another of the straps with his artificial hand. His shoulders suddenly came free. He sat up, fought off a wave of dizziness, and unbuckled the straps around his hips, knees, and ankles. He rolled over and fell painfully onto the concrete floor. The bed trundled on without him, under the machine's scanners, which searched up and down in puzzlement while a big metal claw prodded the empty sheets.

For a moment, he lay on the floor getting his breath back. Then he struggled to his feet. He dodged another mobile bed carrying an unconscious patient. He looked around for a way out, and saw a metal ladder leading to inspection catwalks above.

Jackson started climbing the ladder. His new leg kept wobbling and twitching under him, and it made a nasty clanging noise on the steel rungs. He wondered if there was any chance of getting his old body parts back. They probably kept them frozen in the basement somewhere. No, the main thing was to get the hell out here. He shivered, wishing he had some clothes.

He reached the catwalk and started along it toward some doors that led out of the vast mechanized operating theater. It was lucky the human staff weren't on duty yet. There'd be no one to stop him. He pushed the doors open and stepped through, into a hallway.

He saw some lockers, wrenched one open, and found a mechanic's overalls inside. He pulled them on quickly, trying to avoid looking at the artificial flesh of his left hand. He felt a twinge from his back, and hoped the new kidneys weren't going to start acting up.

Suddenly, he heard voices.

Jackson froze. He peered cautiously around the door of the locker. Two figures were emerging from a doorway farther down the corridor, clutching large boxes stamped MEDICAL SUPPLIES: PROPERTY, BELLEVUE HOSPITAL. Jackson cursed under his breath. He hoped they wouldn't come in his direction. But then, as he watched the figures, he realized they were moving as furtively as he was. His old cop instincts told him there was no doubt about it: these people were breaking and entering.

Impelled by a reflex that went all the way back to his days as a patrolman, his arm twitched, reaching for an imaginary gun. His prosthetic hand jerked and touched the locker door with a dull clanging noise.

The intruders heard the sound and turned quickly. They stared at him. One of them was a hoodlum in a black leather jacket, skintight jeans, and funny pointed shoes. The other was dressed a little more normally, but the face was highly distinctive. The dreamy blue eyes, the blissed-

out expression . . . "You, robot!" Jackson shouted. "Hold
it right there! Freeze!"

"Run," said the one in the leather jacket. "Come on,
Burt, run!"

They disappeared through an exit. Jackson chased after
them, down two flights of emergency stairs. He was getting too old for this game, and his new leg kept doing
weird things. They were well ahead of him by the time he
made it onto the street.

He blinked in the sudden dawn light, and saw he was on
an access road at the back of the huge hospital complex.
The hoodlum and the robot were jumping into an antique
automobile parked at the curb. It was crammed full of
boxes. Jackson ran after them, but the car moved away,
easily outdistancing him.

At the end of the road it made a sharp left, doubling
back toward the river. Puzzled, Jackson ran to a fence at
the side of the street and peered over the edge. He saw the
car swerve around some concrete posts and bump onto a
disused pedestrian plaza. It plowed through some garbage
and drove down a crude wooden ramp that had been laid
from the plaza to a flat-bottomed metal barge in the stag-
nant water. The car stopped, the hoodlum jumped out,
hauled the ramp onto the barge, did something with the
rear wheels of the car, and water started churning. The
barge moved smoothly away, heading toward the vague
shape of Roosevelt Island, barely visible through the morning smog.

"So that's their plan," Jackson muttered to himself. For
a moment, he considered calling police headquarters and
tipping them off. But on second thoughts, better not. He
didn't trust Breen, didn't trust Sanchez—didn't trust any
of them, in fact. To win at this game—bring in the robot,
hang onto his job—he was going to have to crack the case
on his own.

II. GO WITH THE FLOW

"Hey you, hey mister! I got 'em, you want 'em?"

Crosby ignored the guttural voice shouting to him above the babble of the East 42nd Street bazaar. He stood outside the exit of the Chrysler Building with his eyes tightly shut and turned slowly, like a radar dish, searching for Melanie's aura on the psychic waveband.

"Hey, mister! Fresh and tasty, I got 'em right here!"

Crosby thought he almost had it—a brief, tantalizing mental picture of Melanie out there somewhere in New Jersey. But the old hobo kept shouting at him, and there was street noise, and grit had gotten into his sandals, and stray hairs from his ponytail kept blowing into his face.

"Mister! You want 'em?" The hobo nudged Crosby's stomach with his supermarket cart.

Crosby opened his eyes. "Back off, man," he complained, fingering the withered paw on the chain around his neck. "I already got more rat than I can use."

The old hobo assessed Crosby's obvious lack of money and stealable possessions. He grunted, spat into the dust, and moved on.

"Bummer," Crosby muttered. He pressed his fingertips against his forehead, muttered his mantra a few times, then did a Silva Mind Control exercise to refocus his consciousness. He sensed toxic engrams in his brain, triggered by having seen the old hobo's wriggling cargo in the supermarket cart. To avoid permanent trauma, he must neutralize the engrams as soon as possible, preferably by means of health-giving vapors from his special herbal blend, home-grown in his window box on the forty-ninth floor.

He extracted his hash pipe and a pinch of crushed leaves from a pouch tied with a thong to his belt. He lit up and inhaled deeply. His slumped posture began to straighten; his eyes opened wide; he sensed dormant brain cells flashing into life—possibly burning out, it was hard to tell.

Okay, he decided, skip the psychic waveband, the main thing was to move on out before some other piece of urban weirdness freaked him again. He stashed his pipe and shouldered his satchel, loaded with rice balls, Zen koans, and useful pharmaceutical products. Time for action. He stumbled forward into the path of a passing Asian peasant. "Hey, man, hold on a minute, which way to the Hudson River, man?"

The peasant was bent under a wooden yoke. Five-gallon Civil Defense ration cans dangled from it, sloshing half-full of murky gray liquid. "You wan' buy drinking water?"

"No way, man. I got all the diseases I can use right now, thanks."

The peasant eyed Crosby with inscrutable hostility, then pushed past without another word.

Hell, Crosby thought to himself, this was going to be even tougher than he'd expected. He scratched his beard and walked unsteadily across the rubble, between two shacks built from old mainframe computer cabinets. He skirted a chicken pen and came upon a coolie greasing the axle of his rickshaw with a lump of lard. "Hey man, you want to take me to the Hudson River?"

The coolie methodically replaced the wheel on the axle, then straightened up and gave Crosby an indifferent look. "You got money?"

"Money?" Crosby hadn't touched, seen, or thought of money in ten years. The commune traded for all its supplies, and that wasn't his thing anyway. He didn't even have State Food ID.

"You don't got money . . ." The coolie turned away.

"All right, I'll give you my sandals. See this? Genuine

vinyl, man, handcrafted. In your line of work, you need good shoes, right? What do you say, man?''

The coolie inspected one sandal, then beckoned for the other. He gestured for Crosby to get in the rickshaw.

''All right, far out, let's go.'' Crosby made himself comfortable in the old automobile seat lashed between two bent bicycle wheels, and the coolie picked up the shafts. Soon they were moving through the bazaar, crunching and bumping along the street. Maybe, Crosby decided, this wasn't going to be so tough after all. You just had to trust cosmic destiny and go with the flow. If he was meant to find Lennon's runaway chick, he would; and if he wasn't, he wouldn't. Might as well take it easy, in which case a little more herbal mixture wouldn't hurt.

A few minutes later the rickshaw jerked to a sudden halt. Crosby tumbled onto the asphalt, totally stoned. He blinked in confusion. ''Where am I?''

''River.'' The coolie pointed to a stretch of fetid water.

Crosby stumbled over to a crumbling stone parapet. ''Outasight, but I just remembered, I got to make it to New Jersey. I mean through the tunnel, you know?''

The coolie was backing off. ''I go.''

''No, man, I need the *tunnel.*''

The coolie grinned, showing three teeth. ''No tunnel, mister.'' He turned and hauled his rickshaw away.

No tunnel. Probably collapsed or something. Crosby stood on one foot, then the other, imagining deadly Third World bacteria in the filth of the sidewalk invading his body through the unprotected soles of his feet. He wished he hadn't given away his sandals. He hauled himself up to safety, on top of the wall, and sat with his legs dangling over the opposite side.

Maybe he wasn't meant to reach Melanie, after all. In which case, he wondered how long he had to hang out here before he could reasonably show his face back at the commune. Another few hours, he guessed. Well, the time would pass faster with a little grass to help it along. He extracted a generous pinch from his pouch.

Five minutes later he was nodding out. ''Better be

careful, man," he told himself. "In your condition, you could easily fall in the goddamn river." Slowly, he moved to straddle the wall. It wasn't easy; he felt as if he were swimming through treacle. He rotated himself with exaggerated care, then slid off.

He realized he must have made some sort of mistake as he felt the air rushing past, saw the sky turning, then landed with a heavy thump on his back, on top of a massive pile of fishing nets. With difficulty, he figured out he was now in a fishing boat moored in the river, directly below the wall where he'd been sitting.

Crosby sat up, felt dizzy, and lay back down. Screw it, he might as well stay where he was. Go with the flow, right? In fact, he might as well burrow into the big pile of nets like some sort of clumsy, spastic lizard and hibernate there for a while, where nobody would hassle him.

The water lapped at the sides of the boat, rocking it gently to and fro. Crosby was exhausted from his excursion into New York, and he was quickly getting accustomed to the stink of old fish. It was too early for him to be awake, anyway.

One hour later, he was sleeping and safely hidden when the peasant people boarded their boat and cast off. He continued sleeping as they sailed to the middle of the river, dropped anchor, lifted the big bundle of nets (which seemed oddly heavier than usual), and dumped them over the side.

12. LOVE CLINIC

Melanie paced restlessly among the strange machines. She paused beside a microwave oven with the motor from a vacuum cleaner bolted to its side, and leaned against a washer-drier coupled with a Roto-Rooter. Wires trailed everywhere; there were struts and levers and dials, and strange-shaped metal plates nailed to odd parts of the walls and ceiling. Yesterday evening, the machines had worked miracles in modern medicine; today, without Burt's magic touch, they stood idle and meaningless.

Melanie sighed. She studied her reflection in the chromed case of an old toaster-oven. She had washed her hair and was wearing her favorite pink Capri pants and a sleeveless white blouse with a turned-up collar. But this too meant little in the absence of the man she yearned for.

She heard footsteps and felt a pang of hope and apprehension. "Burt? Mick?" She ran out to the top of the emergency stairs—and there they both were, climbing the stairs toward her, carrying big brown cartons. "Oh, thank goodness you're all right!"

"No sweat, doll." Mick winked at her. He walked into the room, dumped his cargo, and flexed his shoulders. "It was a breeze."

"We obtained all the necessary supplies," said Burt, setting his load beside Mick's. Then he walked over to her, took her hands in his, and kissed her on the forehead. "I have a gift. It was Mick's suggestion." He went to one

77

of the boxes, ripped it open, and came back with a bundle
of white cloth.

Melanie unfolded it. It was a nurse's uniform and cap.
She felt tears prick the corners of her eyes. "How wonderful! I always used to dream of being a nurse, caring for the
needy and healing the sick. Now we can have a real clinic
here. People will come from miles around, for Burt to
wipe away their pain. It will be a place of hope, and
love. . . ." She trailed off, realizing her imagination was
running away with her. There was a moment's uneasy
silence.

"All right, I can see you're like on Cloud Nine," Mick
told her. "But there's a couple little details. For a start,
some guy saw us in the hospital."

"Oh no!" Melanie exclaimed.

"He is a policeman, I think," said Burt. "The same
man who was in charge of the other policemen walking in
New York with me yesterday."

"But what was he doing at the hospital this morning?"

"It don't add up," Mick agreed. "He was wearing
overalls, like a mechanic. At first I figured it was a
stakeout, but there weren't no other cops around, and we
got away clean."

"Did he see which way you went?"

"I figure there was too much morning smog," said
Mick. "Still, I'm gonna head back to my place. I got
some infrared binoculars on the roof. If I see anything, I'll
come right on down." He pulled his comb out of his
pocket and ran it through his hair a couple of times. "Till
then, hang loose, okay, sweetheart?" He grinned at her
and strode out.

Melanie sat on the stack of cartons. She clasped her
hands nervously. "Burt, do you think they're looking for
you?"

"I am sure they are. I am valuable to them. But even if
they come to the island, Melanie, they cannot trace me. I
have suppressed the radio beacon which they implanted."

"You what?"

He went over to her, bent his head, and pointed to his

ear. "You see the thin scar there? Feel the earlobe. There is a little lump inside. It is a tiny radio beacon." He straightened up. "I became aware of it yesterday, when I flew into the sky. I quickly stopped its broadcast."

"My goodness! How did you do that?"

He shook his head. "I do not know. I turned my thoughts, *so*. Now they cannot track me."

Melanie was listening him with wide eyes. "Burt, is there *anything* you can't do?"

He gave her a strange smile. "That, I do not yet know."

"Well, you can't live without food," she told him. "I know that much." She stood up and took his hand. "Come along, you must be starving. I'm going to cook you a good breakfast."

She led him through disused corridors to a storeroom that the old hobos had helped clear for her after the party the previous night. They had set up a little kerosene stove, an oil lamp, and a bed improvised from chair cushions. There was no window, but one of the old men had found a 3-D picture, which Melanie had hung on the wall. It showed pine trees, mountains, and a stream that flowed in eerie, perpetual slow motion.

"Make yourself at home," she told Burt. She lit the lamp and the stove, then emptied a couple of ration packs into a frying pan made from an old hubcap.

"Why, this is quite comfortable," he said. "More comfortable than the room Mick gave me last night."

"I can be a real good homemaker." She gave him a shy, coquettish glance.

"I am sure you can," he agreed.

"All I need here is some music," she went on. "Too bad there's no electricity for my phonograph."

"But electricity is all around us," said Burt. "It is in the fabric of the whole universe. We need only the right antenna to receive it. One moment." He walked quickly out the door, then came back a minute later with a weird-looking spiral of wire that Melanie had noticed attached to one of the machines downstairs. He twisted the ends of the wire around the power plug of the phonograph, and set it against the wall. "Which record do you wish to hear, Melanie?" he asked her.

"Just like that? Terrif!" She pulled out a 45 of Elvis singing "I Wanna Play House with You." Soon, the little room was alive with sound.

Impulsively, she sat beside him on the simple bed. "Oh Burt, I couldn't bear it if they locked you up again." She put her arms around his neck. "I wish—I wish we could both fly away, just the two of us. . . . We'd have to cure all the sick people first, of course," she added hastily.

He stared into space, as if there was something only he could see. "One day, Melanie," he told her slowly, "we truly will have to fly away. And that day may come sooner than you expect."

13. GUILTY UNTIL PROVEN INNOCENT

His artificial leg kept clicking and twitching as Henry Jackson limped past sampans, dhows, and barges moored along the waterfront. Some were being used as homes by whole families of peps, in squalor that made him want to puke. Others were being made ready for a day's fishing. Jackson eyed them hungrily, seeing each boat as a potential passport to Roosevelt Island—where, even now, he was convinced the missing robot must be hiding. But even if he could steal a boat, he doubted his ability to sail it.

He hobbled along a jetty that had been lashed together from driftwood and rusty automobile panels. He glowered at the fishermen jabbering in their primitive dialects. With one fone call to headquarters he could get a platoon down here, commandeer the whole filthy fleet if he felt like it, and throw the owners in jail if they were stupid enough to complain. It was too bad he no longer trusted the police department. Until he found out who was out to get him, *everyone* was under suspicion.

Finally, Jackson saw his chance. A little old Chinaman was bringing his rowboat in to the end of the jetty, almost hidden from view by the high gunwale of a fishing junk. Jackson chuckled nastily to himself, unzippered the shirt of his overalls, took it off, and held it loosely between his hands. Dank morning mist settled on the pale flesh of his chest, but he hardly noticed. He quickened his pace along the jetty, concentrating his whole attention on his victim.

The old man shipped his oars, moored the boat, then turned around to pick up a bag of belongings. Jackson leaped forward. His feet thumped onto the thin planks and the boat rocked crazily, tipping the Chinaman onto his face. Jackson fell down on top of him, floundering around. More by luck than judgment he managed to wrap his shirt around the man's head. Quickly, then, he gathered it at the neck and held it with the unnatural strength of his prosthetic hand. There were muffled complaining noises, and the Chinaman started struggling.

"Shut up or I'll kill you," Jackson told him.

The struggles subsided.

Jackson undid his belt with his free hand, wrapped it around the man's neck a couple of times, and buckled it tightly to secure the improvised hood. He paused a moment, lying on top of his prisoner and panting heavily. His heart was racing and his hands were shaking. He licked his lips nervously, imagining himself suffering a coronary here in this wretched little rowboat on the filthy, stinking East River. What if that pseudo-doctor had been telling the truth, and he really did have heart cancer?

Jackson shuddered and pushed the thought away. He struggled up onto his knees, rummaged through the Chinaman's bag of possessions, and pulled out a piece of frayed rope. He quickly tied the man's wrists behind him. "I should do the city a favor and dump you in the river."

He pulled his prisoner up onto his knees. "But as a police officer, they tell me I have an obligation to uphold the law. Even laws invented by *assholes* to protect *parasites*." He kicked the man, making him tumble forward, half out of the boat and onto the jetty. Then Jackson seized his legs and pushed him the rest of the way, behind a stack of lobster traps. "Stay there, understand? Don't move."

He untied the boat, glanced quickly around, and pushed off. No one seemed to have seen anything, and the Chinaman would probably lie quietly for a while. The peps still had some respect—well, fear, to be precise—for people who spoke English.

Now for the hard part. Jackson had never rowed a boat in his life. He sat down, grasped the oars, leaned forward, then pulled back.

One oar dug in too deep, while the other barely skimmed the surface. Jackson yelped with surprise and tumbled over backward, cracking his head on the bottom of the boat. He groaned and lay there for a moment, cursing Third World primitivism.

The rowboat drifted out to the center of the river. Jackson clambered back onto the seat and discovered that a strong tide was taking him rapidly away from the island. He cursed again, and heaved savagely at the oars. One of them dug in especially deep and came out of its crude notch in the side of the boat. Before Jackson knew what had happened, the oar twisted out of his grasp and was gone.

He clutched his head in his hands. There was his oar, floating in the water—drifting away, out of reach. He seized the other oar, kneeled down, and tried to use it like a canoe paddle. The rowboat rocked crazily and started turning in circles.

Jackson scowled at peasants watching him from nearby fishing vessels. He knew better than to ask their help. He imagined drifting helplessly down the river, out into the ocean. Waves would come pounding in; his boat would capsize; the icy depths would drag him down—

But wait. He saw something in the river, close by the

floating oar. He squinted into the brown mist. Someone was actually swimming out there. And he had a Caucasian complexion, praise the Lord. "You!" Jackson shouted. "Get that oar!"

There was a long moment's pause. Finally, the swimmer responded. "This oar, man?"

"Yes, yes!" Jackson cried excitedly.

"Do my best, man." The swimmer grabbed the oar and started making his way slowly toward Jackson's boat. Within a minute, he was close enough for Jackson to seize the oar out of his hands. "Get in," Jackson ordered. Already, a new plan was forming in his head.

The swimmer pulled himself in and shook water off himself like a dog. He wiped his mouth on the back of his hand. "Ugh. That river's pure poison, man."

Jackson observed the long hair, beard, strings of beads, faded caftan. Some sort of aging weirdo degenerate, he concluded with distaste. "What the hell were you doing, swimming with your clothes on?" He made it sound like an arrestable offense.

"Peps threw me in, man." He wiped his hair out of his face, then raised two fingers in the peace sign. "My name's Crosby."

"It's lucky for you I happened along." Jackson paused to let that sink in. "Now *you* can help *me*." He leaned forward confidentially. "I'm a police officer on undercover work—a special assignment, classified, involving national security. Do you understand?" His hard gray eyes stared steadily at Crosby.

Crosby struggled to assimilate the new information. He was still eighty-percent stoned. He groped for his pouch of herbal mixture, figuring that the situation would be easier to deal with if he could get back into his more usual hundred-percent condition. He pulled out a pinch of sodden marijuana, then froze. "You're a cop?"

Jackson nodded slowly.

Crosby didn't doubt Jackson's claim. The fuzz could show up anytime, anyplace, in his experience. A skinny old guy in mechanic's overalls and no shirt, in a rowboat

in the river? Anything was possible. Why not? He *looked*
like a cop, sure enough. Crosby stuffed the grass quickly
back into his pouch.

"What's that you have there?" asked Jackson.

"Nothing, man. Just some herbal tea."

"All right, hand it over."

"Oh, weird," Crosby complained. "I don't believe
this."

"Come on!" Jackson reached forward, grabbed the pouch,
and ripped it off Crosby's belt.

"Just a little grass, man," Crosby whined. "It's nothing."

"Narcotics," Jackson corrected him. "And more than
two ounces, by my estimation. That makes you a pusher.
You realize, under the laws of New York State, there's a
mandatory jail term? Yes, it's still on the books."

Crosby groaned some more.

"However," Jackson went on, "I'm willing to make a
deal. Have you ever rowed a boat?"

Crosby stared at him, trying to adjust mentally. "Well,
hell, I used to live in Malibu. I used to be a surfer, man.
Sure I can row a boat."

"My hand"—Jackson pointed to the prosthetic implant—
"is malfunctioning. As a result, I cannot carry out my
assignment, which requires me to row this boat to Roosevelt Island. You understand?"

Crosby frowned. He looked around. "What island?"

Jackson pointed into the thick brown mist.

"You serious? That's like a mile upriver."

"Your choice," said Jackson.

Crosby looked at Jackson holding the pouch of grass.
He looked at the river. Wearily, he moved to the middle of
the boat and picked up the oars.

Jackson made himself comfortable and watched with
satisfaction as Crosby started rowing. "Chrysler Building," he said suddenly. "I knew I'd seen freaks like you
someplace in the city. Seem to recall we raided it for drugs
and pornography, back before that neighborhood went to
hell. A whole shitload of long-haired creeps in there, isn't
that right?"

Crosby gave Jackson a guarded look, and said nothing.

Jackson smiled. "You know, if I had my way, dope-dealing degenerates like you would be behind bars for life."

"Hey, cool it, man." Crosby paused and wiped sweat off his forehead.

"Keep rowing!" Jackson snapped. "Else the tide will take us right back where we started, and you'll be in big trouble."

"Okay, okay, I hear you." Crosby worked at the oars some more. "Look, I got to get to New Jersey. I'm like searching for this runaway chick. She split from her old man, you know?"

"New Jersey?" Jackson's eyes narrowed suspiciously. "You're a little out of your way, aren't you?"

"What do you mean? It's right there." Crosby nodded toward the opposite shore.

"That, my friend, is the borough of Queens," Jackson told him with a patronizing sneer. "Didn't you learn anything in high school? I suppose you were too stoned. Either that, or too busy sodomizing twelve-year-olds."

"Hey, get off my case, man! This guy, this rickshaw coolie, he told me this was the Hudson River. How was I supposed to know?"

"A mistake anyone could have made," Jackson agreed. "Provided he was an ignorant creep such as yourself."

"Look, cut it out, man! You want me to take you to the island or not?"

"Well, now, that's your decision," Jackson said smoothly. "You row us to the island, or you can take a little ride downtown."

"Yeah? A ride in what?"

Jackson slapped the empty pocket of his overalls. "I have a comm unit right here. Want me to call headquarters? I hope you realize, if I have to get reinforcements to deal with you, that blows my cover on this assignment. And since this is a matter of national security, they'd book you for *treason*. Know what the penalty is for treason?" He idly drew his finger across his throat.

"Bullshit!"

"Try me," said Jackson with a beatific smile. "Just try me."

Crosby glared back. He opened his mouth, closed it again. "Goddamn pigs," he said finally. "Always giving people a hard time."

"Giving people what they deserve," Jackson corrected him. "Do you know what my motto is? Guilty until proven innocent. And even if they're proven innocent, keep 'em under surveillance. Because *everyone* has something to hide. There's not a citizen anywhere who hasn't broken the law sometime in his life."

"Then maybe there's something wrong with the laws," Crosby blurted.

Jackson shrugged. "That's not my department." He lay back and made himself more comfortable. He hadn't felt so content in days.

Finally, half an hour later, they reached the island.

"All right, ease up," Jackson told Crosby. The rowboat was starting to plow through a matted layer of congealed garbage and miscellaneous filth that had accumulated near the shore.

Crosby didn't hear. He had retreated inside himself, pulling mindlessly on the oars, aware of nothing else.

"I said ease up, dummy!" Jackson shouted. Too late: there was an ugly scraping sound of wood against rock.

Jackson jumped to his feet. Putrid water started surging in through a split between two boards in the bottom of the boat.

"What's happening?" Crosby stared dumbly at the water bubbling up between his bare feet.

Jackson stepped hastily onto a nearby boulder.

"Hey, we're sinking, man!" Crosby stood up unsteadily, dropping the oars. He imagined hideous toxins in the foamy scum, seeping into his unprotected flesh. "I gotta get out of this." He scrambled onto some rocks, then leaped to the shore.

Jackson followed, favoring his nonprosthetic leg. He

caught up with Crosby and grabbed his arm. "You realize there's no other way off this island?"

"Hey, man, it wasn't my fault."

Jackson tightened his grip. "You are going to find some way to fix that boat, understand? Just remember, I know where you live." He marched Crosby across a beach of sodden gray mud, up a gentle slope where rubble lay scattered amid tall brown grass.

"Where are we going?" Crosby complained.

"I have an assignment."

"You mean some sort of bust?"

"I am pursuing a fugitive."

"Yeah? Bank robber or something?"

Jackson stopped abruptly and stared closely at Crosby. "Why all the questions?"

"I don't know, I just wondered." Crosby tried to pull back.

"What's your game, mister?" Jackson bared his teeth. "Just a drugged-out hippie, eh? Eh?" He shook Crosby by the arm. "Who are you really working for?"

Crosby shook his head. "I don't work for anyone. I mean, like, I don't work."

Jackson laughed humorlessly. "All right, come on."

They reached the top of the slope. Ruined buildings lay ahead. Burned-out empty windows gaped black. Jackson surveyed them cautiously, then sidled forward, pulling Crosby with him.

"What's that ahead?" Crosby pointed toward the tall, dark silhouette of Fun City.

"We'll find out." Jackson moved toward it with exaggerated caution.

Together, they paused outside the ruined lobby. "Seems to me," Crosby said, "I can smell food cooking."

Jackson sniffed the air. Reluctantly, he realized Crosby was correct. "All right, we'll check it out," he said. "But you're coming too, understand? If this is a setup, you'll be right beside me." He stepped cautiously onto the sodden carpet covered in broken glass, crept around the edge of the lobby, and kicked open the emergency-exit door. "This way."

They paused at the bottom of the concrete stairwell. Faintly, somewhere above, music was playing. Del Shannon, singing "Runaway."

"Man, I just lost my appetite," said Crosby.

Jackson picked up a broken piece of steel pipe that had once been part of the bannisters of the emergency stairs. He prodded Crosby with the end of it. "You'll come along with me, mister."

"But that's plastic-people music," Crosby complained. "Bad vibes. Sweaters with letters, all that shit. This chick Melanie I was telling you about, she used to listen . . ." He trailed off.

"Go on!" Jackson prodded him again. "What about her?"

"Nothing, man, I forget what I was saying. It's nothing." He glanced at Jackson, glanced up into the dark stairwell, then suddenly took off up the stairs, two at a time.

Jackson stared after him. "Hey!" he shouted. "Come back!"

Crosby's footsteps disappeared, up one flight and then the next. A door slammed.

Jackson's knuckles turned white where he held the pipe. He started up after Crosby, his feet scattering fragments of fallen plaster. He reached a door, groped for its handle in the semidarkness, and jerked it open with a crash.

Birds were singing. An antiseptic breeze caressed his face.

Jackson blinked. He stared uncomprehendingly at the forest glade in front of him. Sunlight dappled the plastic grass. He took a step forward, and the turf sank under his feet.

Jackson paused and glanced quickly left and right. His face twitched. He thought he heard something. He dropped down clumsily behind a fake tree. He listened. There! He was sure he heard it that time. A distinct rustling noise.

He started crawling on his belly. There were more

sounds, just ahead. The hippie didn't know the first thing about survival. He'd never served in Vietnam, that was for sure. He didn't understand about kill or be killed.

Jackson stalked his quarry with manic intensity. He tracked him to some fake bushes. All right, this was it. He got a good grip on the pipe and scrambled to his feet.

A tall shape suddenly lunged toward him from out of the foliage. "Give me some cheese!" cried Cheerful Chicken. It made a horrible squawking, clacking sound. "I'm hungry!"

Jackson stared blankly for a moment, then yelled with inarticulate fury. He brought the pipe down on the bird's metal head.

"Quark!" said Cheerful Chicken. He started lurching around in circles.

Behind Jackson, there were running footsteps. He cursed, turned, and strode back to the emergency stairs. He heard the hippie running up one more flight, and went up after him—into the upside-down room.

Jackson saw the furniture attached to the opposite wall. He grabbed the side of the doorway for support. His head was throbbing. His mouth tasted of dirt. Smelly old men were sitting on the wall that was the floor, drinking wine out of plastipacs and wolfing down State Food rations. Crosby was picking his way between them and running out of a door on the opposite side of the room. Jackson took a deep breath, started forward, and stumbled on the tilted floor. His leg hummed and twitched. "Damn you!" he yelled at the old men all around. He brandished the steel pipe. "Get out of my way!" Whiskery faces turned and stared as he blundered among them, finally managing to get to the opposite door.

He found himself in a place full of bizarre machines. Crosby was dodging around them. "Halt!" Jackson shouted.

Crosby ran like a panicked rabbit, out of another door.

Jackson went after him, into a derelict hallway. There was another emergency exit just ahead. Ancient rock music was echoing down the stairs, and Crosby was climbing them two at a time. Once more, Jackson gave pursuit, up

and out along another corridor. The smell of cooking was
stronger here, and the music was coming from a room at
the end. Crosby was heading for it, his bare feet slapping
on the floor.

He burst into the room at the end of the hall, just as
Jackson caught up with him and seized the neck of his
caftan.

"Melanie!" Crosby exclaimed, his eyes on a demure
teenager in pink peg slacks scooping soyburgers out of a
hubcap on a kerosene stove.

"Crosby!" She stopped in surprise.

Jackson looked from one to the other, then saw the third
person in the room. "You! Robot!" he shouted, letting go
of Crosby. "Hold it right there!"

Burt jumped to his feet and tried to make it to the door.
Melanie screamed.

Jackson raised the length of pipe, then remembered the
robot was worth a trillion dollars. He cursed and threw the
pipe down. It hit the floor, bounced with a clang, and
caught Burt across his shin, tripping him so that he fell flat
on his face.

Melanie screamed again. She clutched at Crosby. "Oh
my goodness! Help him!"

"Help who?" said Crosby, genuinely confused.

Jackson leapt onto Burt's back, grabbed his head and
started banging it against the floor. Burt squirmed around
and threw Jackson off. The two men scuffled in the dirt.

"Leave him alone!" Melanie screamed. She kicked
Jackson ineffectually, then seized his leg and started trying
to pull him away.

Jackson hardly noticed. His head was a jumble of obses-
sions: revenge, justice, blood lust, and simple panic. He
clawed at Burt, grunted, gasped, made strange keening
noises, and banged Burt's head against the floor some
more, vaguely hoping to knock him unconscious. Burt was
in far better physical shape than the aging police chief, but
Jackson was like a mad dog. Burt punched him in the
chest, but Jackson didn't seem to feel it. He hit back,
scratched, gouged, and bit. Burt yelped in surprise and

pain. Jackson grabbed his head and pounded it some more. Burt gasped and subsided, his struggles weakened, and his eyes fell half-closed.

"No!" Melanie cried. Once more she tried to pull Jackson away.

He grabbed the steel pipe that he had dropped, and swung it at her. The end of it hit her stomach. She gasped and sat down hard on the bed.

Jackson turned to Crosby. "How about you?" he asked, breathing heavily. "You want to assault a police officer in his line of duty?"

"Hell no." Crosby backed away. "I mean, make love, not war. I'm a pacifist, man."

"I'm not," said a voice.

Jackson turned quickly. Mick was leaning against the door frame, chewing gum, his hands stuffed idly in the pockets of his leather jacket.

Jackson struggled up onto his feet. His naked chest was smeared with Burt's blood. His eyes were wild. "Get out of my way, punk."

"Hey, take it easy, daddy-o," Mick told him with a smile.

Jackson swung the pipe. Mick caught it, pulled it out of Jackson's hands, and threw it into the hallway. He moved forward easily, jabbed Jackson in the face and then the stomach, picked him up and tossed him against the wall. There was a nasty dull thud as Jackson's head hit the plaster. He slowly slumped down in a heap on the floor.

For a moment the only sound in the room was the jingling of zippers on Mick's jacket as he combed his hair.

"Thank you!" Melanie cried. She jumped up and embraced him, and kissed him on the cheek. "Oh, Mick, you were wonderful!"

"Anytime, doll." He nodded at Burt. "He okay?"

"I hope so." She dropped to her knees and helped Burt to sit up. His face was covered in scratches and bite marks. His nose was bleeding and his ear had been mauled.

Mick stepped across to Jackson, who was stretched out unconscious. "This cat don't look so good. Guess I hit

him too hard.'' Mick checked Jackson's head where it had
struck the wall. Already a large swelling was forming.
"So this is the cop, huh? Same guy who saw us in
Bellevue. Must've followed us out here. I saw a rowboat
in the river.''

"That was him and me,'' said Crosby. "He made me
row him here.''

"Oh yeah?'' Mick studied him. "What's your name?''

"Crosby is a—a friend of mine,'' Melanie explained.
"From the commune. Crosby, what are you *doing* here?''

"Lennon sent me. Look, uh, he said to tell you it's
cool, come home, no one will hassle you, you can do your
own thing.''

"But how did you know where to find me?''

Crosby shook his head. "I didn't.''

While Melanie tenderly bathed the abrasions on Burt's
face, Mick propped Jackson up and shook him. "Hey,
cop, how come you were in the hospital? It was you that
saw us there, right?''

Jackson blinked, but his eyes remained unfocused and
his breathing was labored. "Power corrupts,'' he mumbled, "and absolute power is absolute pleasure.''

"This cat has flipped out,'' said Mick.

Burt stood up shakily, wiping blood from a cut on his
forehead. "Who are you?'' he asked. "Can you hear
me?''

"More laws, less justice.'' Jackson grinned and started
to drool.

"What are we going to do with him?'' said Melanie.

"When you got 'em by the balls . . .'' Jackson began.
His eyes fell slowly shut and he slumped forward.

Burt checked Jackson's pulse. "He is alive, but I think
he has severe concussion. I do not know how to cure
that.''

"Dump him in the river,'' said Mick. "That'd take care
of the problem.''

"No!'' Melanie exclaimed. "Two wrongs don't make a
right. We should take him to a hospital.''

Mick laughed derisively. "Sure, fix him up so he can come after us again."

"But Melanie is correct," said Burt. "We do not have the right to take a man's life. He may not be evil. He may simply be misguided. As for his finding us again . . . I believe we must leave here as soon as possible."

"You think there's other heat coming down?" Mick asked.

" There is no way of knowing if this policeman acted alone," said Burt. He looked at Crosby. "Is it true that Melanie's father wishes her to return home to the large building full of people with long hair?"

Crosby nodded. "Absolutely. Right on."

"No!" Melanie objected. "I don't ever want to go back!"

Burt patted her on the shoulder. "I will come with you. Provided you agree, Mr. Crosby."

"Sure, that's cool. But call me Crosby, man."

"I won't go!" Melanie insisted, stamping her foot.

"It will be safer there," said Burt. "Perhaps just for a while. And perhaps your father has truly had a change of heart."

Melanie sniffed back a tear. She rubbed her eyes. "I was so happy here. And what about Mick? What'll happen to him?"

"Mick will take us to Manhattan in his car, on the raft," Burt said. "Then he will drive the policeman to the hospital. After that, he will do as he wishes. I am the one wanted by the authorities. He has nothing to fear."

Mick stood up and dusted his jeans with his hands. "Got it all figured, huh? You been elected President or something?"

Burt shrugged. He gave his serene smile. "I simply know what is best." There was a new tone of conviction in his voice—a sense of eerie certainty. It seemed to make Mick reluctant to challenge him any further.

14. SUPERIOR LIFE FORMS

The Chief Programmer paced the expanse of his underground office, hands clasped behind his back, shoulders hunched, his dark countenance creased by an intense frown. Charlotte followed him faithfully to and fro, her black knee-length high-heeled boots tap-tapping over the platinum parquet floor. She was naked under a black negligee and carried a large bowl of watermelon, from which she delicately spooned small portions into her mentor's mouth whenever he paused and turned toward her.

It was the Chief Programmer's regular habit to ponder and pace in the afternoon, but today his introspective fugue seemed to last longer than usual. "What's on your mind, hon?" she asked finally, tilting her head to one side and batting her eyelashes quizzically.

"Failure," he murmured. "Failure of will. Failure of purpose. Failure of the human species. Failure to *survive*."

"Maybe you should listen to one of your tapes and play with your insects," she suggested solicitously.

He paused. His shoulders lost some of their tension. "Yes," he agreed. "Of course, you're right. Get rid of the rest of that," he added, gesturing at the dish of melon.

She dumped fruit, dish, and spoon down a nearby disposal chute, then followed him across the huge room. One wall of it was covered in hundreds of monitor screens displaying an ever-changing mosaic of global statistics and surveillance pictures. Another wall was taken up with storage cabinets crammed full of tapes, disks, microfilm, and memory chips—the Chief Programmer's personal databank, packed with information on the life of every world citizen above peasant level. On the third side of the room was his recreation area: computer terminals arrayed on three sides of a huge square bed, beside a glass-doored display cabinet full of bondage devices. Lastly, the fourth side of the room was taken up by the Chief Programmer's private research projects. It was to one of these that he turned his attention now.

"Give me tape F-345-0087," he remarked. The environmental-management computer heard him and obeyed. Soon, from concealed loudspeakers came a succession of tormented screams. The Chief Programmer was an avid collector of torture transcripts—tapes of interrogations administered by secret police and military dictatorships worldwide. The sobbing of the victim, intermittently punctuated by the thudding of fists and the crunch of bone, seldom failed to buoy up his spirits.

"I've been neglecting you, my little ones," he murmured, peering into a series of large sealed tanks recessed into the wall. They were full of huge cockroaches, brown chitinous bodies surging up against the glass. The sound of scrabbling legs and busy mandibles was faintly but distinctly audible.

"In the history of the planet," he said to Charlotte, his arm circling her slim waist, "no species has been more successful than the cockroach. Why? Because it is the most *mechanistic* of all living creatures." He absentmindedly pushed his hand up under her negligee and kneaded one of her heavy artificial breasts. "There is no life form superior to it," he went on. "With the exception of you, my dear, of course," he added tactfully.

She giggled and kissed him on the cheek.

He tapped a couple of code numbers on a control panel. There was a distant hissing, and a small quantity of brown gas seeped into one of the tanks. After a moment, the cockroaches began moving erratically, twitching and writhing, scrambling over one another in panic. Hundreds succumbed to the gas and fell on their backs, their legs waving feebly. The Chief Programmer chuckled with affection. "Survive, my little ones," he told them. "Become immune to all known poisons." His breathing became labored as he watched the writhing bodies. The screams on the torture tape, meanwhile, were becoming steadily more anguished. He grabbed Charlotte's negligee and ripped it off with one sudden sweep of his arm.

A melodic chime interrupted this erotic overture.

The Chief Programmer swore softly. "Stop the tape," he commanded. He ran a shaky hand through his Afro. "Who is it?"

"Commissioner Breen, sir," the room system informed him.

"Breen," the Chief Programmer muttered, lips pulling back from his teeth. He strode to a console beside his bed. "Yes, Commissioner?"

"Ah, good afternoon, sir, and sorry to bother you." The man's face appeared on the screen, smiling hopefully.

"Yes?" The Chief Programmer thrust his hands into the pockets of the silver robe he was wearing.

Breen's smile faded uncertainly. "We, ah, have found the missing robot, sir. The radio beacon came back online a short while ago, and is currently located on Roosevelt Island, a small enclave of derelict housing that is located—"

The Chief Programmer was already keying up a geographical readout on another terminal. "I have the data," he interrupted. "Is the robot moving?"

"No, it seems to be stationary, sir. I have given orders to go in with our special forces as soon as—"

"Wait." The Chief Programmer rubbed his jaw meditatively. He glanced over at the tank of roaches, where survivors of the gas attack were already feasting on the bodies of the victims. He smiled faintly. "Assemble your men on both sides of the river, opposite the island," he said. "As unobtrusively as you can; I want this kept out of the media. Just a couple hundred men, including at least a dozen marksmen with high-velocity rifles, and landing craft for the river crossing. Get equipment from the National

Guard if necessary; I authorize it. But do *not* move in, understood?''

"Yes, sir." Breen looked puzzled, but too nervous to ask any questions.

"I'm coming there in person," the Chief Programmer continued. "I'll supervise the operation tomorrow morning. We'll wait till then, provided the radio beacon continues to operate, and provided the robot does not change its location. If the beacon goes down again or moves, contact me immediately. Got that?''

"Contact you immediately if the beacon stops working or moves," Breen echoed him.

"Very good, Commissioner. Very good indeed."

"Thank you, sir." Breen bobbed his head ingratiatingly.

The Chief Programmer cut the connection. He shed his robe and donned street clothes: a leisure suit of funereal black. "Put on your red dress, baby," he told Charlotte. "We're going out tonight. To New York City."

"How exciting!" she squealed with delight.

Minutes later, they boarded his private elevator. It lifted them from the total security of his office, more than a mile underground, to the next level, where management of world affairs was conducted by a select group of government officials totally under the Chief Programmer's control.

He emerged from the elevator with Charlotte, into a small gray room. Armed guards sprang to attention and escorted him as he paced quickly past a series of unmarked doors. He reached the main exit, and paused while scanners verified his identity.

"Hey! Hey there!" a voice shouted from behind him.

The Chief Programmer closed his eyes for a moment. His lip twitched.

"Heck, I been trying to get you on the internal phones, and some cockamamie voice keeps saying you're not home. I knew darned well you were home."

The Chief Programmer heard ex-President Sullivan's heavy footsteps approach relentlessly behind him. He turned quickly. "I have no time—" he began.

"This is important," Sullivan cut in. He glared at the

Chief Programmer's guards as they moved their hands warily to their weapons. "Cut the crap," he told them. "How many times do we have to go through this?"

"Relax. He's harmless," the Chief Programmer told his guards with a weary voice.

"Well now, that's better," said Sullivan. He moved his shoulders uncomfortably under the faded cloth of his shabby three-piece pinstripe suit. He stepped closer, stinking of stale cigars. "I been wondering," he went on, "about next week's World Council meeting. You know, I could use a little outing. Stretch my legs, say howdy to some of the members I knew from back when—"

"You want to take a trip? You can come along right now," the Chief Programmer interrupted impatiently.

"What's that?" Sullivan blinked.

"We're leaving for New York. They found the robot. It could be . . . interesting, for you."

"Well, now. Well, now. Haven't laid eyes on New York since the campaign of '04. Skyscrapers still standing, are they? Hey?" He grinned.

"Most of them. Come on, the plane's waiting."

"Well, well, this is unexpected," said Sullivan as the scanners verified him and the exit door swung slowly open on massive hinges.

"Think of it as a going-away present," the Chief Programmer murmured, in a voice so low that the ex-President seemed not to notice.

15. MISSING MARBLES

Mick guided his Toronado along First Avenue, bumping over lumps of concrete and mounds of garbage. He drove slowly through a puddle the size of a small lake where the highway had subsided into the old sewers beneath, and glared at his passenger sitting beside him. "I gotta have a screw loose, taking a cop to the hospital," he said, shifting the transmission to Low as filthy water splashed around the car. He reached the far side of the puddle, stepped hard on the brakes to dry them out, and watched Henry Jackson rock to and fro like a nodding puppet.

"Give me back my marbles," Jackson complained, lost in a world of his own.

"Would if I could, daddy-o," said Mick. He sighed. It had been too much of a hassle already, driving Melanie, Burt, and Crosby to the Chrysler Building. When running his black-market oxygen, Mick always kept to the avenues. The crosstown streets were mostly blocked with heaps of refuse and mobs of moody, jabbering peasants. He'd told Burt to rig up some sort of super-science gadget to *fly* the car to the building, but Burt had just smiled mysteriously and said he didn't have the proper materials. The guy was a space cadet; full of bright ideas, but no way to get them organized. Anyhow, Mick had delivered them safely, and then Melanie had made him *promise* to take the cop on down to Bellevue.

"If you don't give me my marbles," Jackson went on in a high-pitched childish whine, "I'll break your arm."

"You are one wiggy cat," Mick told him.

The statement seemed to pull Jackson partway out of his stupor. He blinked at Mick. "All right, you," he said suddenly, in his normal adult voice. "Let's see your driver's license." He tried to move his arm, and looked down in confusion, discovering that his hands were tied behind his back. He struggled ineffectually for a moment, then slumped sideways on the seat. "Severe penalties," he muttered as his eyes glazed over again.

Mick finally reached the hospital complex. He stopped at the guard post outside the ambulance entrance. "Guy here got hit on the head," Mick told the robot admissions clerk. "Needs help."

"Please state your Medical Identification Number," the clerk said in a synthetically friendly female voice.

"He can't talk," said Mick, clapping his hand over Jackson's mouth as the cop started reciting some long-lost childhood nursery rhyme. "He's a police officer, you dig? He got, uh, Major Medical and like that."

"Fingerprints, please." The robot's arm telescoped out of its cubicle and into the car, bearing a plastic tablet.

Mick pulled out his switchblade, cut the cord binding Jackson's wrists, and pressed the man's fingers against the sensitized plate.

"Welcome to Bellevue," said the robot after a second's pause. "Where your health is our highest priority—always!"

"Thanks," Mick muttered. The heavy metal barrier swung aside, shedding rust—his was probably the first old-style automobile to have driven up in a couple of years. He moved the Toronado forward.

Faintly, through the open window, he heard a voice shouting something. He looked in his rearview mirror and saw a woman waving her arms, running after the car. Some sort of nut, he decided, probably wanting to get in the hospital, have her bunions operated on or whatever. Mick ignored her and drove through to the ambulance bay.

He hauled Jackson out and pushed him into the arms of a stretcher robot. "Mommy . . ." Jackson blurted as the robot's padded arms gently lifted him. "Mommy, I hate your guts."

"Careful you don't drop him," Mick told the robot. He turned, jumped back in the Toronado, and drove out the exit.

The woman ran in front of him. He saw her just in time and hit the brakes, screeching to a halt. Mick swore. She was the same one he'd seen in the mirror. Fat, middle-aged, in a flower-print dress and a fancy hairstyle.

She slapped her hands on the hood of the car. "What have you done with my husband!" she yelled at Mick. She banged the car with her first.

"Hey, cool it!" Mick jumped out. "Don't mess with that paint job, lady!"

"My husband!" Her rage subsided suddenly into pitiful sniffles. "You took him in there!"

Mick paused and examined her carefully. Didn't normally see her type around town; they stayed out of sight in their underground apartments. Looked as if she had money, he judged. "What's your husband do for a living, ma'am?" he asked, keeping his face blank.

"He's a policeman," she said, sniffing back tears. "Why did you take him in there? Who are you?"

"You're sure it was him I had in the car, huh?" Mick spoke softly now, regarding her with interest.

"Of course I'm sure."

"Here. Sit down a minute." He opened the passenger door.

Carefully, she seated herself. She glanced at his car as if assessing its value. Then she studied Mick's face. Her little eyes made quick, darting movements. "You still haven't introduced yourself to me, young man," she told him.

" 'Scuse me," Mick said. He gave her his best friendly grin. "I'm Michael Verrazano, at your service, ma'am. I saw your husband on the street being robbed by a couple of peps, ma'am. They were really working him over. So I rescued him and brought him here to the hospital. You say he's a policeman? I'm glad I was able to help one of New

York's Finest. There's so little law and order in the city these days." He looked at her with wide-eyed sincerity.

"Well, that's certainly true." She relaxed visibly. "My name is Cynthia Jackson." She held out her hand, and Mick took it with a little bow. "Thank you, Mr. Verrazano, for doing the right thing. Was he seriously hurt?"

"He'll be out of here by tomorrow, way I figure it," said Mick.

"Tomorrow!" She frowned. "After he got me to come all the way down here, and I risked my life on the streets— what am I supposed to do till tomorrow?"

Mick leaned into the car. " 'Scuse me," he said, reaching for a small metal cylinder. "Seems like you could use something to steady your nerves." He handed the cylinder to her. "Try a little . . . oxygen."

"Why, thank you," she said primly, raising the rubber mask to her face. "This is just what I need."

16. COSMIC CONSCIOUSNESS

"So then I hear this fifties music, man," Crosby was saying. "I think—Melanie used to get off on stuff like that! I flashed on it, you know? So I ran like up the stairs, into this trippy kind of a place, a fun house, I mean like an amusement park inside a building. The old guy, the pig, comes after me, he's freaked by the special effects, so I make it through to Melanie, who's in a room with *him*" —Crosby nodded toward Burt—"but then the pig gets ahold of me. I tell him, back off, man, no one comes between me and my sister, you know? Nobody! Well, I mean, I'm a nonviolent kind of a guy, but by the end of it, let's just say they had to take the cop to Bellevue, and here I am, and here she is.''

He grinned proudly as the audience broke into applause. All two thousand of the commune members had gathered in what was once a restaurant on the fiftieth floor of the Chrysler Building, and was now an assembly hall for be-ins, happenings, and rock concerts. Mellow late-afternoon sun slanted through the grimy windows. The sea of hairy heads was half hidden by a haze of dope smoke.

"But Crosby," Melanie protested as the applause slowly died down, "that wasn't the way it happened at all!"

"It does not matter," Burt said quietly, sitting beside her and patting her arm.

Melanie shrugged his hand away and turned on him. "Whose side are you on, anyway? I told you I didn't want to come back here."

"Shh," he told her. "Everything will soon become clear. I sense it."

Lennon had stood up in front of the crowd. He waved his hands for silence. "Brothers and sisters, this is a groovy scene." There were murmurs of agreement. "My girl Melanie and me, we've been separated by the generation gap. You know, I used to lose my cool." Lennon scratched his stomach meditatively. "I used to say to her, 'I fought on the streets of Berkeley for you. I got tear-gassed by the 'tac squad, maced by the National Guard, when I was in SDS fighting to build a better future. Is this how you repay me, by throwing it all away?' "

Lennon clasped his hands across his broad chest and stared ruminatively at his bare feet. There was complete silence now among the audience of aging long-haired acolytes sitting cross-legged on the floor. "Well," he went on, "I was right, but I was wrong. Our revolutionary struggle was right, and it's still right. One day, people will be free. The revolution will free us all to live in peace together."

"Right on, brother!" shouted the audience.

"But," Lennon continued, "at the same time, I forgot.

I forgot that all you need is love. I forgot that being free means free to do your own thing. I realized this when Melanie left. Now she's back, so I get to apologize. Baby, I was wrong. Forgive me.'' He turned to her and spread his arms wide. .

Melanie felt her eyes growing moist. She scolded herself for being so easily moved by her father's speech. Many times she'd sat in this room and listened to him make dramatic speeches, easily manipulating the dope-brained disciples at his feet. And now he was manipulating her . . . wasn't he?

Yet, despite everything, he was still her father. She stood up. She forced an uneasy smile. "I forgive you, Daddy,'' she said.

Lennon turned back to the throng. "She says all is forgiven!'' he bellowed, in case anyone hadn't heard Melanie's demure pronouncement. "Beautiful!'' He marched across and grabbed her hand. Next thing she knew, he was hugging her close to his fat, smelly old body. His robe fell open, and she found her face pressed against the mystical tattoos on his chest.

Finally, she managed to free herself. "How many years is it since you last took a shower?'' she complained, wrinkling her nose, as the audience burst into renewed applause.

If he heard her remark, he ignored it. "And now I want you all to meet our visitor, Melanie's friend Burt,'' he went on. "I was rapping with Burt this afternoon, before we convened the be-in, and he said as how he's been up against the Establishment. Come out here and tell them what you told me, Burt.''

Burt stood up. He had changed clothes, abandoning Mick's 1950s outfit for a flowered shirt and bell-bottomed Levi's. Melanie didn't approve: he no longer looked as neat and clean-cut as before. But Burt insisted it was important to gain the trust of the commune.

He walked out to join her and Lennon. His face was dotted with Band-Aids, and there was a bandage across his ear and forehead. "Thank you for welcoming us to your home,'' he said politely, warming the crowd with his wide-eyed smile. "I am a . . . stranger in a strange land, is that correct?'' There were appreciative murmurs. "But I must warn you, I am avoiding the police.''

"That's cool,'' someone shouted.

"They were using me for research,'' he went on. "For a long time I was in a laboratory. They tried to get me to reveal secrets, but because I have an impaired memory, I could not tell them what they wanted to know. Now, with help from Melanie''—he beamed at her and put his arm around her shoulders—"I am remembering small things. Already, I can help sick people. I hope that you will let me cure many common ailments. And I hope that if I can stay here a little while, away from the police, I will remember much more.'' He smiled, and smiled some more, and hugged Melanie to him. "Thank you all so much.''

"Well, now, it's been a while since we had any new members,'' said Lennon. "But I don't think anyone's going to object.'' He paused for a moment, and stared around the room. "In fact, seems to me we ought to take time out to celebrate. I stopped in at Mistress Ursula's pad on the way up here, and guess what? She just brewed a brand-new batch of sunshine. Anyone here want a taste of cosmic consciousness? Hey? Come and get it!''

There were shouts and some cheers, and people started standing up. The scruffy, shaggy mob moved forward. Some of them stopped to say hi to Burt and give Melanie the peace sign, but most were more interested in a huge pitcher on a table being carried to the center of the room.

"I do not understand,'' Burt said to Lennon. "What is happening?''

"Yes, it's a happening,'' Lennon agreed.

"But what is the colored liquid?'' Burt persisted.

"Kool-Aid,'' Lennon told him. He winked.

"It's LSD,'' Melanie explained. "Lysergic-acid-di-something. A drug.'' She shook her head. "You don't want any.''

"You never dropped acid?'' Lennon asked Burt.

"I have never had lysergic acid, no. Is it nice?''

"Nice!" Lennon laughed. "Is *being alive* nice? Come on, we'll give you a hit."

"No!" Melanie cried. She grabbed Burt's arm. "Don't do it! It's a terrible drug, it drives people crazy! That's how everyone here ended up like this. They took LSD, they became flower children, dropped out of school, took off their clothes, and—"

"You," said Lennon, "are making me uptight." He glared at her from behind his beard.

The hippies were getting noisy now, and sounds were coming over the old Muzak system—Donovan singing "Sunshine Superman." Melanie clapped her hands over her ears. "I should never have come back here," she said, her voice breaking into a sob. "I knew it. You tried to ruin my life, and now you want to ruin the man I love!"

Burt stepped quickly between her and her father. "I will calm her," he told Lennon. "Then I will join you with the LSD."

"Groovy," Lennon agreed, eager to back out of a bad scene.

Burt turned to Melanie. "We came here because the police found us on the island," he reminded her. "There was nowhere else to go."

"With your powers we could build our own *castle* someplace!"

He shook his head. "There is still much that I cannot do. And I have a sense—a hunch, you call it?—that I must be here. Just for a short time. I should drink the LSD with everyone, to further win their trust. I cannot believe something that so many people drink can do me any harm, Melanie. I will only take a small sip."

"No!" she cried again.

"My mind is made up. If it upsets you so much, perhaps you should wait for me elsewhere."

She felt as if something wrenched inside her. This was it, she realized—this was what it was like to lose everything that you cared about. Oh, how quickly it was all taken away! And how helpless she was to prevent it! She looked into his eyes, imagining the life they might have led if they had met in another time and another place. There was no swaying him, she could see that. He didn't realize, didn't understand how drug abuse had ruined the minds of a whole generation. He was too naive, that was the trouble.

"All right," she told him, "do what you want." She looked up at him in despair, then turned away and pushed through the long-haired throng.

Burt went and joined the crowd around the pitcher. Ursula was carefully pouring just half an inch of the rich red liquid for each person. They drank it with a dreamy, spaced-out look in their eyes—a look of anticipation.

"You square it with Melanie?" Lennon asked.

"She will be all right," Burt answered evasively. He turned to Ursula. "Some LSD for me, please?"

"Of course." She eyed him with frank sexual interest as she handed him the cup. "Tell me, Burt, has anyone ever done your chart?"

He drank the Kool-Aid and returned the empty cup. "My chart?"

"Your astrological chart, dear. What's your sun sign? When were you born?"

"That is hard to say. You see, although I am indistinguishable from a human being—"

The rest of his sentence was drowned out as a bunch of stoned-out freaks plugged their guitars into ancient amplifiers and started playing some long-lost song by the Byrds.

"Just sit down, tune in, and groove on it," Lennon shouted in Burt's ear. "We'll listen to the music till the acid starts coming on. Then it'll be like a group trip. A ritual, you know?"

"No," said Burt. "I do not know."

"That's cool," said Lennon. He grabbed a woman near him and started dancing.

Burt went to one corner of the large room, sat down on the floor, and put his fingers in his ears. He remained there for the next half-hour, sometimes closing his eyes, sometimes watching the hippies. Many were making out on the floor, shamelessly throwing their clothes off and groping each other. Burt regarded them enigmatically.

The musicians stopped playing, finally, and joined the rest of the group. Burt blinked and shook his head, as if he suddenly had trouble focusing his eyes. He stood up and picked his way through the mass of sprawling bodies till he found Lennon. The guru was sitting in the half-lotus position, contemplating his big toe.

"Excuse me," said Burt.

"What's that?" Lennon looked up dreamily.

"I have to make an announcement," Burt told him.

"Down the hall," said Lennon. "Second door on your right."

Burt shook his head. "No, you misunderstand. I have something to tell everyone."

Lennon looked irritated. "You're bringing me down, man. I was just getting there."

"I see everything clearly now," Burt explained.

"Yeah, yeah," Lennon said wearily. "That's where it's at. Cosmic consciousness."

"Exactly!" Burt exclaimed.

Lennon turned to some nearby freaks. "Burt just achieved cosmic consciousness," he told them.

"Beautiful," one of them mumbled vaguely. The others barely stirred.

"No offense," said Lennon, looking back at Burt, "but around here, this happens all the time."

"It does?" Burt looked confused.

"Yeah, cosmic consciousness is like a part of being. We live a very spiritual existence, man. Did you see God, or what?"

"Definitely not," said Burt. "I do not believe in God."

"Well, give it another half-hour."

"No." Burt raised his voice. "You do *not* understand."

"Bummer," muttered Lennon.

"I see the *whole cosmos*," Burt continued loudly. "And my part in it. I am not a person like the rest of you. I have a human body, but it was grown in a tank. My consciousness, my mind, my programming, came from another star. I am an alien being.''

''Far out,'' said one of the hippies stretched out nearby. ''You come here on a UFO or what?'' Beside him, his girl friend giggled.

Burt compressed his lips to a thin line, and shook his head. ''None of you understands.'' He stepped quickly to one of the guitar amplifiers. The back of its case had long since fallen off or been thrown away; Burt easily reached in and started pulling out pieces of wire and electrical components.

''Hey,'' the owner of equipment shouted. ''Hey, that's my amp, man!''

''I will replace it.'' Burt didn't even bother to look up. He worked quickly, stripping wire with his teeth and braiding it into a complicated coil terminating in an old vacuum tube and a potentiometer. He twisted the knob slowly, and his body became bathed in a strange green glow. Slowly, Burt rose up into the air. The green glow fizzed and pulsed, illuminating the astonished faces of the hippies stretched out beneath. ''Now,'' said Burt, ''perhaps you will listen more attentively.''

There was a confused murmuring as freaks started debating whether what they saw was part of their trips, or real.

''But I didn't do any drugs,'' one middle-aged flower child spoke up loudly. ''And he sure looks like he's flying to me.'' She stood up and picked her way across the room. ''What are you *doing?*''

''A simple demonstration of my knowledge,'' Burt replied. ''I am from a race infinitely older than mankind.''

''Personkind,'' the woman corrected him curtly.

Burt ignored her. ''The LSD repaired my brain damage,'' he persisted, drifting slowly across the room and back, leaving a faint trail of ionization in his wake. ''I remember everything now. My race broadcast instructions from their planet, across interstellar space. Your scientists received these instructions—which were in an easily decipherable, mathematical form—explaining how to build a replica of a human being, based on images my race had received from your television stations. They explained, further, how to program the human being with a vast wealth of knowledge. This was a gift from my race to yours. A way of communicating personally with you without entailing the difficulties of interstellar travel.''

"Are you God?" one of the freaks interrupted.

"No, no, there *is no God*." Burt was beginning to sound testy. "At least, not so far as I know."

"You mean you're not sure?"

"That's a theological question," said Burt. "It is not relevant."

"It's relevant to me, man. I mean, look, here you are, flying around the room, you look like God to me. Doesn't he look like God?"

"Some sort of deity," said Lennon, moving to the center of the room. "Why did you *choose us?*" he asked Burt, his voice touched with awe.

"My planet routinely monitors all radio wavebands, and routinely broadcasts information to all intelligent species," Burt explained patiently. "But something went wrong this time. There was a break in the stream of programming data. I emerged from my tank with amnesia. Now, however, I know everything."

"Everything?" someone asked. "Can you see the future, and like that?"

"I can only sense the future indirectly. However, while I was being programmed, I had free access to the central data banks in the computer of the World Council. The computer that manages all world affairs," he explained, trying to get this point across to the blank faces staring up at him. "I now recall everything—the terrible plan that has been laid for the future of this planet. There is very little time left for us to act, and we may not be able to save the world."

"Armageddon!" someone shouted out. "We're all going to die!"

"No!" Burt shouted back. "None of you will die. We will all be safe. But you must do exactly what I say." He flew over to the Kool-Aid table and drifted down till he was standing on it.

Lennon walked across to him. "You, uh, sure about all this?" He gestured at the crowd of hippies, many of them sitting up now, talking uneasily to one another. "Wouldn't want them to get worked up over nothing, you know?"

"I am certain." Burt smiled ironically. "I truly have cosmic consciousness."

"See, the acid, it can do things to your head," Lennon went on. "Give you hallucinations."

Burt lifted his feet off the table. "Is this a hallucination?"

Lennon walked all around the levitating figure. He slid his hand cautiously under Burt's feet. "Not so far as I can tell."

"Correct," said Burt. "I must apologize for—spoiling your scene? I realize you are an important figure to your group. You are their leader. I do not want to make you seem less important in their eyes."

Lennon laughed without much humor. "Let's face it, there's no way I ever got up and flew around the room. You're the real thing, man. You're the guru now. You tell us what to do, and we'll do it."

"That's right," said a voice. It was Crosby, who had wandered over beside Lennon. "Knew there was something freaky about this dude, soon as I saw him," he said. "Had that spaced-out look. Like from outer space, know what I mean?"

Burt smiled. "All right, let me tell you what must be done," he called to the crowd. "First, we must seal this building so that it is completely airtight."

"Already is," Lennon said. "We keep the smog out that way."

Burt shook his head. "It must be made perfect, so no outside air enters at all. Next, I will show you how to construct flying devices like the one I have made here, but much more efficient. You will go as emissaries into the outside world. You will bring items of importance back here. I will explain the details tomorrow, when the LSD

drug has worn off and you are able to concentrate on what
I have to say.''

There was a confused response.

"You do what he tells you," Lennon shouted to his
followers. "This dude is the real thing.''

"What else?" Crosby called up to Burt.

Burt switched off his flying device, and the green glow
faded. He jumped down from the table. The crowd moved
back as if afraid to touch him.

"I must go to Melanie," he said. "Reassure her of my
state of mind, and tell her the many things I have learned.
I sense that she and I will share much together.''

No one tried to stop him as he walked quickly across the
room.

17. SON OF MAN OF PARTS

Henry Jackson opened his eyes. A woman on the huge TV
screen in front of him was sobbing, slumped over a kitchen
table. A tall, handsome man had his arm around her
shoulders. "Laura," he was saying, "I have to know.
What happened to our baby?"

Jackson groaned.

"Ask me anything else, Mark," Laura begged him.
Organ music surged in the background. "Anything. I'll—
I'll even tell you about my affair with Janet.''

"You and Janet? Then it's true!" He collapsed into a
chair. "You and my twelve-year-old mongoloid sister. Oh
God."

"But don't ask me about your baby.''

"Doctor!" Jackson shouted feebly. "Nurse!" He closed his eyes, trying not to believe he was back in the hospital again.

"Laura, what have you *done?*" Mark's voice trembled with emotion. It seemed to bounce around inside Jackson's skull. "You didn't . . . take it to the postnatal disposal facility?"

"Mark, you forced me to have that child, even though there isn't enough to eat and there's no room in the world for more people. It was wrong, Mark, wrong!"

"Stop it," Jackson mumbled, half in and half out of a coma. "I can't take it." He opened his eyes in time to see Laura falling helplessly into Mark's arms.

"Maybe you're right," Mark was saying. "Maybe I was selfish." He stared suddenly into the camera. "There *are* too many mouths to feed, and we should all remember—"

Mercifully, the screen went blank and the sound died. Then a face appeared that was all too familiar.

"How are you doing, Henry?"

Jackson took slow, deep breaths, trying to summon what was left of his inner strength. "What did you do to me this time?"

"You're a lucky man, Henry. Yes indeed."

Jackson twisted in his straps. "You did something to my body. It feels heavy, and stiff."

"You'll soon get used to that, Henry." The doctor's face smiled warmly. "And you'll live to thank us for it. With what we've done for you, you'll live an extra thirty years."

"But what—"

"You were readmitted in very serious condition. Hardly surprising, after you discharged yourself against our orders yesterday."

"The robot!" Jackson's mind began to clear. "I apprehended the robot, but then—"

"Severe exhaustion," the doctor was saying, "Irreparable damage to vital organs. Frankly, your old body couldn't take that kind of punishment."

"My *old body?* Wait a minute. What the hell is that supposed to mean?"

"From the outside, you still look much the same. But inside, you are a showpiece of modern medical technology. All organs have been replaced."

"*All* of them? You mean, even my—my—"

"Well, you still have one testicle. If you wish, we can make an appointment to take care of that sometime next week."

"You bastards!" Jackson felt overwhelmed by the enormity of it all. He swallowed hard, and his throat felt weird. Everything felt weird. There was a hot sensation in his chest. A whining noise in his ears. His heart was beating at half its normal rate. He groaned in anguish. "Just tell me who," he begged. "That's all I ask. Who instructed you to do this? I can die in peace if I know who—so long as I get to take him with me." He clenched his fists. Something about the action made his body vibrate disconcertingly for a moment, like a tuning fork.

"Little too much negative feedback in your neuromuscular system," the doctor observed. "There's a simple screw-adjustment to fix that. You can take care of it yourself. Routine maintenance."

"Oh God," Jackson moaned.

"Henry, you've got to get ahold of yourself. It's pointless to feel sentimental attachment for worn-out flesh. Do you realize how lucky you are? You'll never have to eat again!"

"My stomach?"

"The whole abdominal cavity. You don't even need to breathe. Imagine, Henry. An atomic reactor small enough to fit inside your ribs. Incredible, isn't it?"

"I'll deal with you later," Jackson said feebly. "Just let me out of here."

"We should really keep you under observation—"

"No! Goddamn it, let me go!"

The doctor's features froze momentarily as a remote system processed Jackson's case history. Then the face reanimated itself. "Okay, Henry, just sign our standard release form.'' A thick wad of paper covered in micro-scopic print emerged from a slot beneath the TV set. The straps retracted from Jackson's right arm. A pen was presented to him by a telescopic metal rod. He reached for it and saw his new prosthetic hand. Well, at least the left one and the right one matched each other now. He squinted at the form, but the print all blurred together. Fatalisti-cally, he scrawled his name at the bottom. Tiny servomo-tors whined in his wrist; the signature came out totally illegible.

A metal claw plucked the contract from Jackson's grasp and dumped it down a chute. The bed reared up under him suddenly, forcing him into a sitting position. The metal claw dumped a massive book into his lap: *Operating Instructions for Super Prosthetic Torso, Kadukiyawa Robotics Corp, Tokyo.* Below the title, in big red letters: *Important! Failure to observe correct procedures voids your warranty!*

Jackson lifted his head to scream abuse at the face on the TV screen, but the screen had gone dark. The bed lurched under him, nudging him forward so that his feet landed on the floor. With dim gratitude he noticed they'd allowed him to keep his old original right leg.

Doors of a recessed closet hummed open, and an auto-matic hanger presented him with the police uniform he had been wearing on the day he had first been admitted to Bellevue. Jackson saw the blue cloth and felt like crying, but his eyes stayed dry. Artificial eyeballs, he realized. No need for lubrication. The tear ducts had been removed.

He looked down at his naked flesh. There was a fantas-tic webwork of red scars, and his body was lumpy. He felt it with his prosthetic fingers. There were odd angular *things* just beneath the skin, throbbing with a rhythm of their own. Around his navel he discovered a fissure in the skin, like the edges of a small, square trapdoor. He looked more closely, and saw that the navel had been replaced with a flesh-colored plastic locking screw, with a little label tattooed beside it: ''Do not open. Refer repairs to authorized personnel. No user-serviceable parts inside.''

Numbly, Jackson dressed himself. The uniform didn't

fit properly anymore, and there was no sign of the combat suit he had been wearing over it on that fateful day. He buckled his gun belt; that, finally, made him feel slightly better. He imagined confronting the criminal who had somehow arranged for this to be done to him. Imagined a .44-caliber bullet plowing into the felon's face. Imagined the skull exploding and the brains spattering.

No, that would be too easy. Jackson located the exit from the tiny room—a small door opposite the hatchway that had opened yesterday when he had been trundled into the operating theater. He opened the door and emerged into a sterile hallway. He hardly saw it; he was imagining his tormentor tied to a chair, at his mercy. A billy club was in his hand—although, come to think of it, he wouldn't even need a billy club. His plastic fist would do just fine. And if it was true he didn't need to eat or breathe anymore, he'd have unlimited stamina. The brutal punishment could last for hours—days, even!

The thought cheered Jackson somewhat as he hobbled unsteadily along the corridor, following Exit signs.

Yes, revenge would be sweet. First, of course, he had to find the felon. And before that, he still had to deal with the problem of the missing robot. Close that case, get his job back, then commandeer the full resources of the police department to track down the culprit. Tap phones, subpoena records, beat up suspects in jail cells, bribe officials—the whole standard procedure. It wouldn't take long if it was managed right.

By the time he emerged through a one-way revolving door into the main hospital lobby, he had begun to feel cautiously optimistic. The lobby was crawling with human filth: peasant people suffering all kinds of disgusting degenerative diseases, from boils to beriberi. They were pressing themselves against an armor-glass window, beseeching a robot nurse to allow them into the hospital. Some had collapsed on the floor and seemed near death. Jackson stepped over the bodies with disgust. He used the strength of his new right arm to push the rest of the peasants out of his way. "Police officer," he snapped at them. "Stand aside!"

Soon he was outside the main pedestrian entrance. He blinked. It was early morning. The question was, Which morning? He grabbed a passing coolie and flung him against the hospital wall. He drew his gun and nudged the man's chin with its barrel. "All right, you. What day is this?"

The man gibbered and rolled his eyes. "Is Wednesday!"

Jackson nodded. He holstered his gun. "Just checking. Stay out of trouble, scum." He sneered and moved on.

So, he'd only been in the hospital one night. Amazing what modern medicine could do, these days, if you had total coverage. He flexed his arms and felt an odd sense of energy pulsing through him. Maybe it was just the psychological effect of having his old uniform back, or maybe it was the reactor in his stomach. He didn't like to think about that too much. He considered the catastrophic consequences if something went wrong. Some sort of meltdown. Better be careful to read that instruction manual.

He realized, with shock, he had left the manual in the hospital room. Well, he could get it later. The important thing now was to stay on top of the case.

He walked quickly around the huge hospital building, reached the access road at the back, and paused a moment. Yesterday's scene was etched in his memory: the two fugitives jumping into their illicit vintage automobile and driving down to the river, onto the raft. Jackson tucked his thumbs in his gun belt. They'd taken round one, there was no denying that. But the game wasn't over yet.

He walked to the primitive dock nearby, where he'd hijacked the rowboat the previous day. He remembered how helpless he'd felt without his uniform, his gun, or even any shoes to wear. Well, things would be different this time around.

He walked slowly past the various fishing boats, attracting suspicious stares from the peasant owners. Finally, he settled on one that looked in better shape than the rest, and was about to cast off. "You there!" he shouted to the swarthy crew. "Hold it. I'm coming aboard."

A few minutes later the ship set sail into the East River, with Henry Jackson's revolver pressed against the ribs of the wizened old captain at the helm. There really was no substitute for the judicious application of force, Jackson mused to himself as the boat took him once again toward Roosevelt Island.

18. GREASER GADGET FREAK'S NEST OF SIN

"Am I alive?"

Cynthia Jackson spoke the words in wonder, blinking at the room in which she found herself. She was lying on crisp, clean sheets in an old-fashioned double bed that had real springs in its mattress. Behind her head were not one but two genuine polyester-filled pillows. On top of the sheets were a blanket and a candlewick bed cover. White gauze drapes over the window were dappled with sun. Below them, an old-fashioned air conditioner hummed gently.

"I declare, I'm either dead or I'm dreaming."

She turned over in the bed and saw an antique bureau with a lace doily protecting its richly polished wood. There were family photographs, and a three-piece mirror. Against the opposite wall was a wardrobe, just like one she remembered from her childhood. The room smelled of lavender and furniture polish.

The door opened and Mick walked in. He had shed his usual leather jacket in favor of a baseball sweatshirt, short pants, and sneakers. He laid a tray on the bed. Cynthia saw fresh scrambled eggs on a porcelain plate, and a tall glass of orance juice. "Morning, Mrs. Jackson," said Mick with a shy grin.

"Wherever am I?" There was a tremor in her voice. "Am I all right?"

"You're fine," he told her. "Seemed like you came over faint yesterday, outside the hospital. The oxygen I gave you didn't bring you around, so I took you back to my place. This used to be my mom's room, before, uh, she went away."

"It's just beautiful." Cynthia picked up her fork and started on the eggs, barely aware of what she was doing. "You say I fainted?"

"Maybe you breathed too much outside air," Mick suggested.

"Yes, of course. I should have known better. All those years breathing filtered air. We moved underground because my husband—" She broke off. "You took him to the hospital, didn't you? I remember now."

"That's right." Mick sat down on the edge of the bed. He studied Cynthia Jackson the way a butterfly collector might examine a particularly interesting new specimen.

"What a kind young man you are." She chewed her eggs thoughtfully.

"Just call me Michael, ma'am." He brushed his hair back from his forehead with a shy, boyish gesture.

"So you—you put me to bed? All on your own?" She noticed she was still wearing her underwear. The idea of his having removed her dress and slipped her into the bed was shocking, yet . . . yet what? There was a strange emotion she couldn't name for a moment. Something she hadn't felt in fifteen or twenty years. She searched her memory. Why, it was *titillation*. She gave him a wary look.

"I'm a strong guy," Mick was telling her. "There was nothing else to do, Mrs. Jackson. I had to take care of you."

Those last few words struck a special resonance inside

her. "I—I'm glad you did," she said. "Tell me, do you by any chance have a mirror?"

"Why, sure thing." He opened the top bureau drawer and took out a hand mirror, brush, and comb. "These are my mom's things, too." He passed them to her.

Cynthia Jackson fussed with her appearance. "She was lucky to have such a nice boy like you."

Mick didn't bother to mention he was forty years old. "So, uh, this takes you back, does it?" he said, gesturing at the room.

She put down the mirror. "I remember when I was a little girl—"

"Like in the fifties?" Mick put in eagerly.

"Yes," Cynthia said cautiously, "it might have been as long ago as that."

"You drove to school in a car, huh?" Mick went on. "You listened to records on the radio, you ate hamburgers and pretzels and like that, hey moms? I mean, uh, Mrs. Jackson?"

She smiled nostalgically. "I had a ponytail."

"That's wild! You gotta tell me all about it!" He edged closer.

She finished her breakfast. "Later, perhaps."

"No, why not now?"

She gave him a stern look. "I'm in a delicate state of health, Michael."

"Oh, uh, sorry." Something about being reprimanded by her seemed to please him even more.

"I need a robe," she said primly. "I have to use the bathroom."

"Sure thing, babe." He took a satin bathrobe from the wardrobe and handed it to her.

"You should call me Cynthia," she corrected him, discreetly pulling the robe over her underwear. "Now, where is the bathroom?"

"Oh. Yeah. Well, see, I kept this room like Mom had it. But the rest of the place is in kind of a mess. See, I'm into cars, and memorabilia, and—"

"The *bathroom*, Michael."

"Okay, I'll show you." He led the way into the hall.

The drivetrain from a pickup truck was right outside the door, along with a pile of broken electric guitars. In the bathroom, Cynthia Jackson found the tub had recently been used to wash out a gearbox with kerosene. "Michael! This place is a disgrace!"

"See, moms—uh, Cynthia—if I'd of known you was coming, I—"

She closed the door in Mick's face.

He hugged to himself, and started pacing restlessly to and fro.

When she emerged, he showed her the patio. She sniffed disdainfully at the smog. "I feel faint again already," she said, and touched a hand to her forehead. "I think I should stay in the bedroom until I am entirely recovered, don't you? That should give you time to clear up this terrible mess."

"Sure thing, Cynthia." He took her arm solicitously. "Don't you worry. I'll take care of you."

Again, those wonderful words! She leaned on him gratefully. "You're so kind," she murmured, giving him a quick, searching look. "You know my husband never really understood—" She trailed off. "I suppose he'll be coming out of the hospital today," she added with vague regret.

"I'll give them a call," Mick assured her. "Check on his condition. Maybe he'll have to stay there longer than we thought."

"You think so? He always did whatever he wanted, you know. Never really took my needs into consideration." She sighed. "Yes, call the hospital, dear. I'd appreciate that. When you have time."

Mick escorted her back to the bedroom. He didn't bother to tell her that the phone lines between Roosevelt Island and Manhattan had been dead for years.

"Maybe you'd like to watch TV?" he asked, helping her back into bed.

"You have a tank?" Her eyes brightened with interest.

"TV tank? None of that shit."

"Michael! Your language!"

"Oh, 'scuse me. No, I got an old color set, and a VCR. We can look at some tapes from the old days. *I Love Lucy, Big Valley, The Love Boat, Dallas,* I got 'em all."

"Well," she said, mollified. "That sounds nice. Perhaps you'd like to sit here and watch some of them with me?"

"That'd be a gas. . . . I mean, sure."

She reached out and patted his cheek. "You're a good boy, Michael."

By the middle of the morning, he managed to get her talking about her youth. "Did you ever wear a ring around your neck?" he asked.

"Why yes, a boy—I forget his name—he gave me a ring to wear."

"I always wondered about that," said Mick. "Must have been a big ring, huh? Did it, like, fit over your head and rest on your shoulders? I never been able to imagine it."

"No, no, silly boy! The ring went on a string, and the *string* went around the girl's neck."

"Oh, so *that's* what it was all about. I been listening to that old Elvis song for years, and wondering, you know? 'Won't you wear my ring around your neck—' " He started singing.

"Well if you give me one, maybe I will," she said coquettishly. "Just to show you how it was done, of course."

"Cool, baby—" He broke off. "What's that sound?"

"I don't hear anything."

"Sounds like a motor. Hold it, I'll be right back." He ran out of the room, along the hall, and onto the patio. Out here, it was clearly audible. Mick squinted around. Finally he saw it, descending through the smog. A helicopter, homing in on the Fun City building.

"This is the police," a loudspeaker blared down from the chopper. "We have the building surrounded."

Mick looked quickly along the shore. At first, he saw nothing; then he made out a few figures stretched out in the long grass, holding rifles. And a landing craft, on the muddy beach.

"We are here to apprehend robot B.E.R.T.H.A., property of the U.S. Government," the loudspeaker blared on. "Come out and surrender. You will not be harmed. You have ten minutes."

Mick could see the way it would go. They'd storm into Fun City. They'd discover Burt wasn't there anymore, then search the rest of the island, just to be sure. That would include his whole setup, bootleg oxygen and all. Maybe they'd take him in, so's not to go home empty-handed.

He ran back to the bedroom. "I gotta split this joint," he told the surprised Cynthia Jackson. "The heat's coming down."

"Whatever are you talking about?" She was chewing a chocolate, watching an old episode of *Family Feud*.

"Look, uh, I don't know how to explain this, but the business I run here, it ain't strictly legal. The cops are on the island looking for some guy, and if they search my place it'll mean time in the slammer for sure. Get me?"

She frowned at him. "Michael, are you on the wrong side of the law?"

"Not exactly. I'll explain to you later. Come on, babe, we gotta make tracks."

"Don't be ridiculous, dear. My husband is Chief of Police. I'm sure he can straighten everything out for you."

"Your old man is *what?*"

"Chief of Police. You have nothing to worry about."

Mick groaned. If Jackson recovered his memory overnight at Bellevue, he'd sure as hell remember Mick as the one who threw him against the wall. Plus, he might not appreciate the way Mick had run off with his old lady. "Look, we don't got time to argue," he told Cynthia. "I don't want to leave you on your own here. Come on, honey. Quick. Do it for me, huh?"

Pleading, cajoling, and nudging her along, Mick finally

got Cynthia Jackson into her clothes and out the door. By this time, the ten-minute police deadline had expired and the bullhorn on the helicopter was ordering cops into the Fun City building.

Mick hustled Cynthia down to the ground floor, where he'd demolished an apartment years ago to make a secret garage for his car. He got her into the passenger seat, ran around to the driver's side, jumped in, and gunned the motor. "We gotta peel out of here," he told her.

"I still say you're being ridiculous," she told him. "And quite inconsiderate." She wore a vexed expression and sat coldly at the far end of the seat with her arms folded. "You know, sometimes I think men are all alike."

"Maybe if I cut around the back, they won't see me go," said Mick. He took the car down a narrow pedestrian path overgrown with weeds, then bumped through an empty lot and around behind Fun City. He glanced in the mirror: so far, no one was coming up behind. With luck, the cops would all be inside the Fun City building by now. He wondered how they'd figured Burt was hiding there.

He swung around the perimeter road. The place where he stashed his raft was just up ahead. He noticed a peasant fishing boat moored at the shore, which was odd—the peps never bothered with the island, normally. Then a figure suddenly stepped out of some bushes, right in front of the car. A cop in uniform. Mick swerved, trying to avoid him, but there was a dull thump and a clang. He lost control, and the car plowed off the road and into the ditch.

The motor died, and everything was suddenly silent. Dust rose in clouds. Insects buzzed outside Mick's open window. The hot metal clicked as it slowly started to cool.

He pushed his door open.

"Don't leave me!" Cynthia Jackson wailed.

"All right, all right." He reached back and pulled her out of the car.

"Michael, how could you do that to me? I almost had heart failure." She clutched her chest. "Oh my goodness. The air! I can't breathe!"

Mick ignored her. He stared moodily at the Toronado,

its wheels in the ditch. Probably not damaged too badly, but it'd take a winch to haul it out.

"He's hurt!" Cynthia exclaimed, looking at the figure stretched out on the road. "Do something, Michael."

"Sure, sure." He turned away from the car. "All right, let's go look at him." He took her arm.

The injured figure managed to sit up as they approached. He was groaning and clutching his right leg where the car had hit it.

"Henry!" Cynthia Jackson exclaimed in horror. "Henry, is that you?"

Henry Jackson looked up. He seemed to have trouble focusing his eyes.

"Your husband, huh?" said Mick. "It figures. The guy has a bad habit of showing up where he's not wanted. Just one thing—" He stepped forward quickly and plucked Jackson's gun out of its holster. "I may need this." He winked at Cynthia. "I had myself a ball, babe. Let's get together again real soon."

He turned and ran, then. The peasant fishing boat was just pushing away from the shore. Mick jumped from boulder to boulder, then made a daring leap, got his arms over the side of the boat, and hauled himself in. "You cats going my way? Like, Manhattan? I got me an urgent engagement. This here's my ticket." He pulled the gun out of his belt.

Wearily, the old captain turned the wheel, and the boat set sail for its return voyage.

19. BZZZZZZ

The Chief Programmer kept the helicopter hovering at two hundred feet, just in front of Fun City. He held the controls in one hand; his other hand hovered over the launch button for a heat-seeking missile.

"Not planning on using that thing, are you?" Sullivan shouted across above the noise of the rotors. "Blow up a trillion-dollar robot? Just like that?"

"If it attempts to escape by air, yes." The Chief Programmer favored Sullivan with a brief, cold glance. He turned his attention to a communications console between the two pilot seats. "Commissioner Breen, come in, please."

"Yes, sir. My men are inside the building. We'll have a video link direct to you any moment, sir."

"You still have a signal from the beacon in the robot?"

"Yes, sir. And it has not moved. It is still located in a room on the third floor of the building. I think we have him this time."

"Good. Meanwhile, Commissioner, I noticed an automobile moving on the perimeter road." The Chief Programmer glanced across at the tip of the island. From his perspective, it seemed that the Toronado was merely parked at the curb. "Send some men to check on it. It's at the south end of the island. It's stopped, and I see two people near it. Bring them in for questioning."

"Yes, sir, right away. And here's your video link."

The screen flickered into life with a picture transmitted from a camera held by one of the cops walking up the emergency stairs. The picture swung and jumped erratically as the man moved through into a corridor on the third floor.

"Wow, this is exciting," said Charlotte, standing at the Chief Programmer's elbow.

"Be a lot more enlightening if you'd explain—" Sullivan began.

"Wait," the Chief Programmer snapped. He leaned forward, studying the screen intently. A booted foot swung into view; there was a moment's pause, and then the foot kicked a door open.

The camera swung around, taking in every detail of a small, windowless room: a kerosene stove, a simple bed fashioned from chair cushions, a tacky 3-D poster of a mountain stream.

"Breen!" the Chief Programmer snapped. "You're sure this is the correct room?"

"Yes, er, it is, but it does appear to be empty." The commissioner's voice no longer sounded quite so cheerful.

"We have the beacon," a cop cut in on the voice channel. The room was filling with uniformed men; one was scanning it with some sort of tracking device. He stooped down, picked up something, and held it up for the camera. The picture blanked for a moment, then switched to close-up.

"The beacon is intact," the voice continued. "Seems smeared with blood. Apparently was ripped out of the fugitive's ear."

"Fresh blood?" the Chief Programmer asked.

"Dried. Looks five, six hours old or more." A cop's face swam into the camera's field of view. "Seems the suspect left the building some time ago."

The Chief Programmer turned away from the video screen. He stared broodingly out at the sky for a moment. A grim, dangerous expression flickered across his face. "Search the rest of the building," he said. "Call in extra men to sweep the island." He paused. "I'm coming down myself."

He flipped the comm switch off, and turned suddenly

toward Sullivan. "Stay in the chopper," he commanded. "I don't want them to see your face. Your presence here would be hard to explain."

"Well, hey, whatever you say," said Sullivan. Something about the Chief Programmer's tone seemed to have rattled him. "But I sure would like to know—"

"Later." The Chief Programmer brought the helicopter in fast. It landed outside Fun City with a sudden jolt. He swung out of the door and marched into the building without looking back.

Half an hour later, the Chief Programmer was lying in the plastic grass, his back against an artificial tree. He held in his hand the miniature radio beacon that had been embedded in Burt's ear. It gleamed in the slanting rays of artificial sun as he studied it meditatively.

"Hello Mick?" said Ronald Rabbit.

"Who programmed you?" the Chief Programmer said quietly, turning his attention away from the little component in his hand.

"Let's go for a walk!" said Ronald Rabbit.

"Some other time." He turned to Mister Mouse. "What about you?"

"Cluck cluck cluck," said Mister Mouse.

The Chief Programmer sighed and moved on to Cheerful Chicken. "Do you have anything intelligent to tell me?"

"Bzzzzzz," said Cheerful Chicken. He stepped forward uncertainly, then slumped to one side.

"Malfunctions," the Chief Programmer murmured. "The world is riddled with them." He absently fingered the dent in Cheerful Chicken's head.

"We found these entertainment devices, ah, hiding in the bushes over there," Breen explained. "Clearly, they had some purpose when the building was in use as a recreation center. They seem to have been recently renovated, which suggests some link with the, ah, homemade electronic equipment we discovered on the floor above."

The Chief Programmer held out the radio beacon to

Ronald Rabbit. After a moment's hesitation, Ronald hopped
forward and opened his mouth. The Chief Programmer
tossed the beacon in and watched the rabbit chew it up,
making a horrible grinding noise.

He turned his attention back to Breen. "You're wrong,
Commissioner. These *devices,* as you call them, were
repaired by a dilettante. Upstairs, we see the work of a
virtuoso. A crippled virtuoso, but a virtuoso nonetheless."

Breen was still standing, not having been invited to sit
down in the grass beside his superior. The forest glade
made him decidedly uneasy. "No doubt you are correct,"
he said diplomatically. "In the meantime, we have questioned the elderly residents of the building, and they unani-
mously claim that the homemade devices cured various
physical ailments." He paused and laughed awkwardly.

"Indeed." The Chief Programmer turned to Cheerful
Chicken. "What do you make of that?"

"Bzzzzzz," said Cheerful Chicken.

Breen cleared his throat. "Should I have that equipment—"

"Don't touch it." The Chief Programmer fixed Breen
with a cold stare.

"Very well, sir. As you wish." He shuffled his feet
some more. "We did bring in the persons you saw by the
automobile, outside."

The Chief Programmer shrugged. "And?" He stared
into Ronald Rabbit's glassy eyes. Ronald Rabbit stared
back, waiting for some verbal cue.

"They are, er, Chief of Police Henry Jackson, and his,
er, wife, sir. I understand he was discharged from Bellevue Hospital just this morning, came to the island on his
own initiative in a somewhat heroic attempt to recapture
the missing robot, but was unfortunate enough to suffer
further injuries when the automobile ran into him. It was
driven by a local resident who fled the scene."

"Poor Mr. Jackson," said the Chief Programmer. "He
hasn't been having much luck lately, has he?"

"Jackson is in extreme pain, sir. I believe he should go
back to the hospital for surgery."

"Good idea," said the Chief Programmer. "Send him back to Bellevue. They'll know what to do."

"But he was eager to have a word with you beforehand."

"He was, was he? Very well." The Chief Programmer stood up to receive his old adversary.

Breen left, and a few minutes later Henry Jackson staggered in. His body bulged oddly under his uniform. His right leg hung at an unnatural angle, and he was using a piece of wooden plank as a crutch. He hesitated in the doorway, eyes darting around as if checking for enemies in the artificial foliage.

"Mr. Jackson," said the Chief Programmer. "Over here."

"Who the hell are you?" Jackson blurted. His face twitched.

"I am the presidential aide in charge of this case."

"You are?" Jackson hobbled forward, grimacing with pain. He eyed the Chief Programmer skeptically. "Didn't see you clearly. Standing in the shadows there, your complexion kind of blended in." He paused and rested against a tree. "Just wanted to explain my side of this," he said. "Want you to know someone has been working against me. From the start. They even got through to the hospital control systems somehow. The bastards have ruined me." He glanced around again, as if expecting an assailant to come up creeping behind him.

"The hospital control systems?" The Chief Programmer shook his head. "That sounds hard to believe."

"They replaced every organ in my body!" Jackson's voice rose to a shrill pitch.

"Do you find it to be an improvement?" He sounded genuinely curious.

Jackson seemed not to hear the question. "I actually had that robot," he rambled on. "Had it, in my hands, but I was unarmed. Some thug hit me, that was the last thing I remember."

"You had the robot?" The Chief Programmer's tone was no longer so relaxed.

"Followed it here yesterday."

"Without reinforcements? That was unprofessional."

"Didn't trust 'em. Not after what they did to me."

The Chief Programmer's eyes narrowed. "I see. So, there was a scuffle upstairs, was there? You struggled with the robot?"

"That's correct, sir."

"Perhaps you injured its face? Might even have taken a piece out of its ear?"

Jackson grinned. "Correct!"

"I see. Let me make sure I understand. You blundered in here yesterday alone and unarmed, sustained minor injuries that enabled the suspect to escape, and then came blundering back here alone again today, just in case the suspect had decided, out of the goodness of his heart, to stay and wait for you to apprehend him."

Jackson shifted his grip on his crutch. "Sir, there were unusual circumstances. As I say, I was unable to rely upon the police department. There are jackals there—" He paused and visibly tried to get a grip on himself. "I was merely attempting to do my duty."

The Chief Programmer gave him an ironic smile and said nothing.

"With all due respect, I feel I should retain my position in the department. Give me that much, and I'll not only get your robot, I'll prove there's been a conspiracy. I'll cut out the rot. I'll clean up the whole festering mess. I'll see the culprits suffer."

The Chief Programmer sighed wearily. "Get a grip on yourself, Jackson." He studied fingernails for a moment. "I realize you have had an unfortunate experience at Bellevue Hospital. However, you obviously need to have that leg fixed up. I give you my personal assurance, if you go back there now, everything will be all right. You'll be dealt with overnight, I imagine. Come back and see me tomorrow, and I'll have a new job for you."

Jackson hesitated. "A new job?"

"I absolutely guarantee it will make you happy."

"But what—"

"Sorry, Jackson, that's all I have to say. Oh—one

thing. You were once a New York City patrolman, weren't you? You had a beat in Central Park.''

Jackson frowned. "Well, yes, I did."

"Just verifying the records. I started out on a low rung on the ladder myself, you know. Token black at IBM."

Jackson gave him a funny look. For a moment, it almost seemed as if the police chief remembered, or recognized . . . but no, he shook his head.

"Get that leg taken care of," the Chief Programmer finished up. "I imagine it must cause you considerable pain." He spoke the last two words slowly, as if they raised nostalgic memories.

"Yes, sir." Jackson grimaced. "Very painful."

"Henry!" a shrill female voice called from out in the hallway.

"My wife," said Jackson. "I'd better go." He started for the door.

Cynthia Jackson got there before him. "Henry! Are you still trying to walk on that leg? Are you out of your mind? Do you want to be crippled for life?''

"You're interrupting a high-level conference," he growled at her. He turned apologetically to the Chief Programmer. "My wife's distraught. Sorry about this. Not her usual self.''

She grabbed Jackson by the arm and hustled him toward the door, almost knocking him off his crutch. "If you have the slightest concern for me, Henry, you'll get them to take care of your leg right this minute.''

"Interesting," said the Chief Programmer, watching them leave. Then he took his compad from his pocket, and dialed into the local data network. He still remembered the Bellevue access codes; it took a matter of moments to enter them on the miniature keyboard.

20. FLESH AND BLOOD

He was outside in the hallway knocking on her door again. She tried to turn up her phonograph to blot out the noise, but found the volume was already as high as it would go. The Shangri-Las were singing "Past, Present, and Future," and Melanie was stretched out facedown on the bed, sniffling, feeling totally desolate.

The knocking persisted, and she heard him calling to her.

"Leave me alone!" she moaned.

The record ended. Burt's voice came through clearly now. "Melanie, you cannot stay in there forever. You must eat."

"I'm not hungry." She reached for "To Know Him is to Love Him," but thought better of it. She stared disconsolately at her record collection. None of the titles appealed to her. Everything seemed empty and meaningless.

"Please, Melanie. I left you alone last night because you asked me to, but today we must talk. Do you no longer care for me?"

"It can never be the same." She blew her nose loudly.

He pounded on the door some more. "Please!"

"Oh, all right, all right!" She stumbled over to the door and unlocked it, then retreated quickly to her bed. She got into it fully clothed and pulled the covers up to her chin as if to shield herself from him.

Burt stepped into the room. "Melanie, you don't understand." He closed the door carefully behind him.

"I understand that you—you're a—a monster." She sobbed some more. "And all this time, you deceived me."

"I tried to tell you, even on the island, that I was different from other people." He sat tentatively on the end of her bed.

She shrank away from him. "Different? You're not a human being at all! That's if I believe what you said last night. For all I know, the acid trip made you crazy. I don't know which is worse. It's a nightmare. I can't bear it."

He patted her leg, under the covers. "Please—"

"Don't touch me!"

"I have flesh and blood just like you," he insisted.

She stared at him doubtfully.

"Look." He picked up a nail file from her bedside table and stabbed it suddenly into his fingertip. "You see?" A blob of blood slowly formed.

The sight of him hurting himself stirred something in Melanie. She tried to hold it back. "You told me . . . you said that inside, you're not a person."

"No, no. That is not correct. I am as much an Earth person as you. I just have extra memories."

She sniffled. "You said some scientists *grew* you, in a tank."

"That is true. But premature babies are kept alive in incubators. Is that so different?"

"You don't even have a mother or a father." Her voice was growing smaller each time she spoke.

"I am an orphan," he agreed, smiling at her sadly. He sucked the blood from his finger. "But in this, I am not so different from you. You are estranged from your father, and your mother abandoned you. We are both misfits, lost in space and time."

"Oh, Burt." Her voice was barely more than a whisper. "I'm so confused."

"Please trust me," he told her. "I am a good person, Melanie. I wish to help others. But to do that, I need your help."

She remembered being with him on the island, healing

the old men. He did seem decent and kind, and yet— "So it's not like there's some *thing* in your head?" She swallowed and sniffed. "I mean like those horror movies where there's this thing like a blob that suddenly comes out and—and—"

"Of course not." He gave her his wide, beatific smile. "I have a mind and a body like anyone else. My mind simply knows more." He reached for her hand and held it.

At first she tried to pull her hand free. Then she hesitated. He sensed her indecision, drew her quickly toward him, and hugged her before she could resist.

"Don't!" she cried. "Please!"

"I love you Melanie," he told her.

"How can you say that? You shouldn't say that!"

"I know everything now." His voice had that tone of serene certainty again. He patted her gently. "All I want, Melanie, is for you to stay beside me for the next two days. That is all. It is not so much to ask."

"You just want me to be with you?"

"That is right. So you can make up your own mind." He stood up, took her hand, and pulled her out of bed. "There is so much to be done. I have been up all night making preparations."

"You didn't get any sleep? You mean, you don't need to sleep like other people do?"

"Of course I need to sleep. I am very tired now. But there are important matters. The people in high levels of government will want to recapture me because they fear that, if I have regained my memory, I now know all their plans for the future of the world. Terrible plans, which must never be put into practice. You see, to these people I am a weapon that can either destroy them or, if they can control me, help them in their work."

"Gosh!" She chewed on the tip of her thumb.

"Do not be alarmed. I have the whole commune working for me now. Even your father has pledged his help."

"He has?"

"I convinced him of my powers. We went to the basement and obtained supplies of copper wire and other items.

People are making devices according to my instructions. Luckily, many persons here are adept at handicrafts. Meanwhile, I must secure this building. Won't you help me, Melanie?''

The fiftieth floor had been remade overnight. A production line had been set up on old restaurant tables. Hippies were putting together little gadgets from copper wire, bits of plastic, cloth, and string, following Burt's plans drawn on old ledger pages tacked to the walls. Everyone was working with single-minded concentration.

"I've never seen them like this before," Melanie whispered, standing unobtrusively beside Burt in the doorway. "Except maybe when they were harvesting their dope."

"I have given them a new purpose in life. Look." He pointed to the far corner of the room. As each gadget came off the production line, Lennon picked it up, held it just so, and drifted a few inches off the ground, his body surrounded by a flickering green aura. Then, having tested the item, Lennon carefully added it to a heap in a box at his feet.

"I call those devices *lifters,*" said Burt. "Soon, there will be one lifter for each person in the commune. They will go out across the city, emissaries invulnerable to almost any mortal threat."

"They will? How come?"

"You will see." He led her into the room.

As soon as the hippies saw him, they stopped what they were doing and stared with undisguised awe. Lennon came hustling over; he pressed the palms of his hands together and bowed ingratiatingly. "Peace!" he said, a blissed-out expression on his fleshy face. "Is everything okay? Was the bed we gave you soft enough? Was the food hot enough? Uh, if you don't mind me asking."

Burt smiled beneficently. "My needs are easily satisfied."

"Of course they are, you're a spiritual master, I can relate to that." He glanced at Melanie, then back at Burt. "She still giving you any problems? Need me to talk to her?"

Melanie stamped her foot. "Daddy!"

"Everything is fine," said Burt. "All I wish is that the lifters be ready as soon as possible."

Lennon turned and glared at his workers. "You heard him, keep busy!"

"I require just two lifters now," Burt continued. "Melanie and I must inspect the outside of the building."

"We must?" She looked at him in surprise.

"Yes."

"No sweat," said Lennon. "Here." He hurried back to the box, pulled out a couple of the gadgets, and handed them to Burt. "Anything else you want, you just tell me, right? Peace!" he said again, as Burt smiled and nodded and turned away.

"Why are we going outside?" Melanie asked as she and Burt walked out.

"You will see. But first . . ." He led the way down the emergency stairs, along another corridor, and into Mistress Ursula's room. Here, a huge tangle of wires had been erected around a giant cooking pot that was normally used to prepare the commune's organic rice and lentil stew. Ursula was fiddling with an improvised control panel, her face showing anxiety bordering on panic. The web of wires was fizzing and crackling, and an eerie orange glow was pulsing inside the cauldron.

"Burt!" She looked at him with evident relief. "I was calling to you with ESP. Thank goodness you heard me. Are you positive, dear, that this is safe? Doesn't it force the pattern of things? Aren't we wrong to impose our will on cosmic harmony?" She eyed the equipment with evident distrust.

"No, Ursula. Think of this device as a sailing ship blowing with the wind, the ether wind that permeates our universe."

"Oh." She still seemed doubtful.

"It is part of our destiny," he assured her.

"It is? Maybe I should throw the I-Ching, and—"

"There is no time for that." He stared steadily into her eyes. "We are ready to begin work, here."

"But I still don't understand—"

"It is a converter. It turns one form of matter into another. We will place surplus items into the cooking vessel. From this pipe"—he gestured to a tube crudely attached to the side of the pot—"a fluid will emerge which, when conveyed through the hole in the window, there, to the outside of the building, will form a monomolecular film spreading itself over the entire structure."

For a moment, there was silence in the room, broken only by the fizzing and popping of the electric field.

"It sounds *technological,*" Ursula complained.

"It is good karma," he told her with a smile. "Please begin placing refuse in the pot. Come, Melanie."

They left and climbed the stairs to the old Cloud Club in the spire of the building. An overpowering odor of green leaves, wet earth, and sap greeted them as Burt pushed open the door.

"Hey, man," said Crosby, half hidden among a fantastic new profusion of plant life. He fought his way through the tangle of vegetation and stepped over vines and roots that had burst through the bottoms of the planting pots and were snaking across the floor. "How's it going?"

"It is going well," said Burt. He surveyed the mass of foliage filling the room.

"Where did all this come from?" Melanie asked.

"Beats me," said Crosby. "He took some stems and seeds, you know, and put 'em in some little wire gadget, then gave 'em back to me and told me to plant 'em, and five hours later—" He shrugged.

"I wish there to be fresh green plants in every part of the building," said Burt. "It is time now to take clippings and distribute them."

"Just so long as the plants leave room for the people, man," said Crosby.

"It will be easy to restrict their growth, just as it was easy to enhance it," Burt assured him.

"You're the guru, man. Whatever you say." Crosby hesitated a moment. " 'Scuse my asking, but can I get high on any of this shit?"

"I think not," said Burt.

"That's a drag. Well, I'll get busy with the scissors, man. Bits of green shit in every room. You got it."

"Groovy," said Burt.

"Don't talk like that," Melanie scolded him.

Burt walked out, and she followed him up one more flight. "They expect me to speak as one of them," Burt explained to her. "I am their leader now."

"I don't know why you had to pick them. Why couldn't you find some respectable, decent middle-class people to help you? Why does it have to be this bunch of smelly weirdos?"

"I have little time, Melanie." He pushed open a creaking steel door that gave access to the observation deck—a narrow walkway around the base of the building's spire of gleaming stainless steel. Gusts of smog made Melanie squint and choke. The midday sun was a pale silver disk in the grayish sky. "It might not have been so easy to win the trust of a different group," Burt explained, letting the door slam behind them. "And this building suits my needs."

Melanie blinked. Her eyes were stinging. "What now?"

"Here." He gave her one of the lifters he had received from Lennon. "Turn it so." He showed her a small adjustment.

"What's happening?" Her voice rose in alarm as the tingly green glow curled around her like a blanket of plasma.

"Do not worry. Place the device in your pocket. Now imagine that you are rising into the air. Think of your feet lifting up."

"I don't know. I'm scared, Burt."

"You merely have to synchronize your brain activity. Let me show you." He activated his own device, and drifted easily up above her.

"But what if it goes wrong?"

"It cannot. While the field encloses you, you cannot be hurt by anything. It filters the environment. Already it is easier to breathe, yes? You see, this is a much more sophisticated system than the one I made to escape the police when they first took me out into the city. Try it, now.''

Melanie did as he said. She imagined her feet losing contact with the cracked concrete of the walkway; and she felt it happening. She gave a little cry of fright.

"Here.'' He reached for her hand. There was a slight shock as her fingers touched his, and their green auras merged. "You said you wished to fly away with me, Melanie.''

"Oh!'' The building was drifting away beneath her.

Together, they rose up. The speed increased, but she barely felt the air rushing past—that too was filtered by the green glow. The buildings of Manhattan seemed to shrink, and the sun suddenly became brighter as she and Burt emerged from the smog layer.

"Blue sky!'' she cried in amazement. "Just like in picture books!''

"It appears blue because other wavelengths of light are more easily scattered by particles in the upper atmosphere,'' Burt explained.

"I'm scared.'' She pulled herself close to him.

"As Franklin Roosevelt said, 'We have nothing to fear but fear itself.' Fear is a survival trait, Melanie, in situations comparable to those in which human beings evolved. But here and now, fear is little more than a biochemical distraction.''

She was barely paying attention. "We can see the whole of Manhattan Island!''

"Yes. Strange to think that in 1790, it was the capital city of the United States.''

"Burt, stop it. You're making me dizzy.''

"Dizziness is usually caused by a disturbance to the canals of the inner ear,'' he explained helpfully.

"I said stop it! Why are you telling me all this?''

He paused. "It seems that now I have recovered my memory, I find it hard to stop remembering things.''

"Jeepers, Burt. You're such an egghead. And I know almost nothing about anything.''

He made no response for a moment. Then he moved one

hand behind her neck and kissed her, slowly, gently, and with feeling. Suspended with him in the air, wrapped in his arms, with the strange green radiance pulsing around them, Melanie felt unable to resist.

"I am merely an idiot-savant," he told her a moment later. "I know facts, but facts are all I know. You have so much to teach me, Melanie."

"I do?" She looked up at him with wide eyes.

"Yes. The feelings you inspire, these I do not know. The emotions are not under my control. If only we had more time. But we must go back now."

"We must? How come?" She still clung to him as they started sinking smoothly through the air.

"I must check on the progress of my plans." He said nothing more till they were on a level with the Chrysler Building again. Then he pointed to one of the thousands of windows. "There, do you see?"

Melanie realized it was the room in which Ursula was tending the modified cooking pot. The pipe that went from the pot to the hole in the window was oozing a colorless fluid, flowing out like a thin coating of oil, reflecting rainbows. The puddle it formed was slowing spreading across the brickwork of the building.

"We will soon be safe," Burt told her.

"From what?"

"From our enemies."

They flew lower, hand-in-hand, and Burt studied the rest of the building as if making a map inside his head. Soon they were just a few stories above the ground, and peasant people in the 42nd Street bazaar were shouting and pointing up at them.

"Are *they* our enemies?" Melanie asked, remembering the mob that had pursued her just two days before.

"No, they are themselves victims," Burt told her.

But once again Melanie hardly heard him. "Look!" she cried. "Down there, banging on the main doors in Lexington Avenue!"

"It appears to be your friend Mick," Burt agreed.

"Why do you think he's here? Do you think he needs help?"

"We shall find out." Together they swooped down. "Excuse me," Burt called to the leather-jacketed figure. "Do you want a lift?"

"No doubt about it, pops, that's the only way to fly," Mick said a few minutes later as they touched down together on the observation deck. "Lemme see that." He took the little gadget from Melanie. "This is all it takes, huh? You got it made in the shade."

"Since I regained my memory," Burt said, walking back into the building, "I have made many things. I will be happy to show you. But what brings you here?"

"Need a hideout till the heat dies down," said Mick, following Burt and Melanie down the emergency stairs. "The island's crawling with cops."

"Why is that?" asked Burt.

"Looking for you, dad! Why else?"

Burt paused and turned. A look of surprise was on his face. "The radio beacon!" He touched his fingers to his bandaged ear. "It has gone. And free from my mental field, it must have resumed working. Why, I believe the policeman tore it out of my skin when we were struggling together. Mick, I am sorry."

"Hey, don't sweat it. Not your fault."

"But I should have been aware—"

"Why weren't you?" Melanie asked. "You have all these superpowers, don't you?"

Burt looked embarrassed. "A person with superpowers can still make mistakes," he said.

"That's adorable," Melanie said. She turned to Mick. "You can stay with us as long as you like. Can't he, Burt?"

"Of course." Burt led the way into the main room on the sixtieth floor. "This is where we have been assembling the lifters," he explained.

"Just finished," said Lennon, bustling over. "We made

them all, just the way you said." He beamed ingratiatingly at Burt, and then noticed Mick. "We have a visitor?"

"Yes," said Burt. "A friend from Roosevelt Island. Melanie saw him outside the main entrance, which of course has been sealed, in accordance with my instructions. So we brought him in via the roof."

"What's your sign? Scorpio?" Lennon asked, eyeing Mick's leather jacket and jeans stained with motor oil.

"Who's this wiggy old cat?" Mick asked Melanie.

"My father," she hissed at him.

"Mick is a talented engineer," Burt interrupted smoothly. "He will be helping me here. If you have finished making the lifters, Lennon, it is time to distribute them to the disciples. Each person should practice flying around the spire of the building, until flying becomes second nature. The nervousness will soon wear off. So long as you are enclosed in the force field, you are completely protected."

"I grok you," Lennon answered, beaming again, "in fullness." He turned and started distributing the gadgets to the disciples who had been helping to manufacture them.

"Never did hit it off real big with hippies," said Mick as he walked with Burt and Melanie out of the room and down more stairs.

"Me neither," said Melanie.

"Figure I'll use your pad till tomorrow, then head back home," Mick went on. "Okay, you guys?"

"I will be glad of your help while you are here," said Burt. "And in return, I will give you your own lifter, and other devices."

"Solid," said Mick.

"There is much here that needs to be done," Burt went on, descending yet another flight of stairs.

"Yeah, dad, like suppose we fix the elevators, how about that?"

"Or we could rip them out completely and just *fly* up and down the shafts!" Melanie put in.

"It is not good to use the lifters in small spaces, where the field is confined," said Burt. "And in any case, there are more urgent matters."

He refused to answer any further questions until they laboriously walked all the way down into the subbasement of the building. Here, in a wide, dank, dim-lit space, they found several sweating hippies piling old galvanized garbage cans along one wall and wrapping them with bailing wire, according to plans drawn up by Burt.

"What's with the cans?" Mick asked, shouting above the clanging of metal on metal.

"I will explain in a moment," said Burt. "Here is what I want you to look at." He pointed to a huge stack of ripped cardboard cartons. "When the owners of this building declared bankruptcy, they packed many items, intending to remove them. Some, however, were forgotten. You see these video monitors? They were a closed-circuit security system. The control units and cables are also here."

"Keen," said Mick, sizing up the hardware with a professional eye.

"We will convert this equipment to gain access to worldwide telecommunications," Burt told him. "The spire will be our antenna. Also"—he gestured to a massive telephone junction box against the wall, covered in dust— "that will enable us to tap the local data network."

Mick grinned. "Planning on making some phone calls, huh?"

"If necessary, I will transmit my message to the whole world."

"Yeah? Using what for power?"

Burt smiled enigmatically and gestured at the ranks of garbage cans. "When the coils of wire are correctly adjusted, power will be the least of our problems."

21. INVISIBLE PROTECTIVE SHIELD

The Chief Programmer sat on the promenade by the East River in a chair that had been brought out from Fun City. Wearing a smog mask and wraparound goggles that heightened his habitual air of deviousness and inscrutability, he watched with no apparent interest as two police officers manhandled a bulky gray cabinet toward him along the cracked pavement.

"This is the teleprinter you asked for, sir," Breen explained, standing discreetly nearby.

"Place it directly behind me." The mask gave his voice an ominous, droning resonance. "You have the gasoline generator also?"

"Coming, I believe." Breen indicated a third cop pulling a small machine on wheels.

"Keep that as far from me as possible."

The men set about following his instructions.

"Excuse me for questioning this," Breen put in tentatively, "but our data links are not compatible with this printer. You won't be able to send or receive anything, sir."

"Naturally." The Chief Programmer gestured to the thin silver tablet resting on his knees. "I have my compad for that. I require the teleprinter, Commissioner, purely for the *sound* that it makes."

A few minutes later, the machine came to life and began clattering out line after line of random characters. The Chief Programmer closed his eyes for a moment, allowing the electromechanical rhythms to wash over him. He realized with satisfaction that he could no longer hear the crying of seagulls, the wind rustling through the trees, or the water lapping at the shore.

He pressed a key on the compad and raised his voice. "Charlotte?"

"Hi, hon! Enjoying the sunshine?" Her reply emanated from the compad's small internal transducer.

"Is Sullivan getting restless?"

"Don't think so, hon. He seems happy as a hog with his beer and his baseball quiz, and I just put some more hot dogs in the microwave for him."

"Good. Be sure he stays in the helicopter." The Chief Programmer broke the connection. He scanned the sky-scrapers of Manhattan on the opposite shore, feeling certain that somewhere among those towers, his quarry lay hidden. Sullivan's time was not yet ripe; but soon, soon.

"Sir? We have searched the whole island." Breen's voice intruded above the hammering of the printer.

"And?" The Chief Programmer did not bother to look up.

"No sign of the robot, sir."

"I didn't think there would be."

Breen moved uneasily. "So, ah, what is our strategy, sir?"

"We wait. Our fugitive will show himself in due course."

"I see. Well, whatever you say, sir."

"Yes," the Chief Programmer agreed amiably, "whatever I say." He frowned, then, still scanning the skyline. "Commissioner! What are those *large birds* over there?" He pointed to a scattering of black specks, barely visible, circling one of the skyscrapers. "Have vultures started roosting in Manhattan, feeding on street people who collapse from malnutrition?"

"Not that I'm aware of, sir."

The Chief Programmer shook his head with regret. "A pity. Hunting them by helicopter—with a hand-held laser, perhaps—would make a fine sport."

"Yes, sir, I suppose it would. If you particularly wish it, sir, I suppose we could contact the zoo and arrange—"

The Chief Programmer gestured irritably. "Get me some binoculars."

"Binoculars." Breen sounded weary. "Certainly, sir. Right away."

He came back a few minutes later and handed the Chief Programmer a pair of military field glasses. The silence was broken only by the relentless noise of the teleprinter as the Chief Programmer inspected the distant circling specks in close-up.

Finally, he handed the binoculars back and got to his feet. "I am going over there in person," he said to Breen. "You will activate the comm link we used earlier. I may need assistance." He turned without waiting for a reply, walked to his helicopter, keyed the door open, and stepped inside.

"Ya wrong again, buddy," an offensive male voice was blaring from a loudspeaker in the entertainment console. It gave a wheezing, cackling laugh. "Babe Ruth never hit a homer in Philly. Ya shoulda said Little Tommy Vinciello. Dat's another twenny ya owe me. Wanna play some more?"

"Gosh darn it." Sullivan thumped his fist on the metal panel. "You sure about that? I could have sworn—"

"Save the game for later," the Chief Programmer told him. "We're going up. Better strap in."

Soon the helicopter was lifting off, its downdraft kicking dust into the faces of Breen and his men. The Chief Programmer watched with mild interest as the dwindling figures doubled over, coughing and knuckling grit out of their eyes. Then he turned the chopper toward Manhattan.

"That building"—he pointed ahead—"is the Chrysler Building. Correct?"

"Yep." Sullivan slapped his knee.

"You are a fund of information," the Chief Programmer complimented him. "But what do you make of those figures flying around it?"

Sullivan frowned. He rubbed his nose with his knuckle, coughed, and used his other hand to massage the back of his fat red neck. "Funny-looking critters," he said finally. "No wings on 'em. Don't see how they stay in the air."

The Chief Programmer took the helicopter high over the skyscrapers, cautious of unpredictable thermals and downdrafts. He activated a terrain-scanning system and locked it

on to one of the moving forms beneath. The screen flickered into life, showing a scrawny old man in a caftan
zooming around the towers of Manhattan, his long frizzy
hair blowing in the breeze. He turned, looked directly up
at the helicopter for a moment, grinned, and gave a clenched-
fist salute that the Chief Programmer remembered from
student demonstrations of the late 1960s.

"Flying faggots," exclaimed Sullivan. "I'll be darned."

"Some of them seem to be female," the Chief Programmer pointed out.

Sullivan shrugged. "I can't hardly tell 'em apart, myself."

"They appear to be taking off from that ledge near the
top of the building. Circling around, testing their powers
of flight." He drummed his fingers on the controls.

"Building looks like it's just been repainted," said
Sullivan.

"More as if it has been *polished*."

"Like with one of those silicone cleaners that leaves an
invisible protective shield!" Charlotte put in. "I saw it on
a TV commercial," she added shyly.

"Quite right," the Chief Programmer told her. He moved
the helicopter back from the circling hippies. "How's your
trigger finger, Sullivan?"

"Ah, what's that? Eh?"

"Think you could bag one of them?" The Chief Programmer gave him a bland, inquiring look.

"One of them long-haired weirdos?" The ex-President
fingered his jaw. "Don't know as how that seems constitu-
tional, if you'll excuse my saying so."

"Those people don't vote, Sullivan. They're social
parasites."

"Hrmph. Ah, you may be right. But nevertheless—"

"Oh, very well." The Chief Programmer quickly armed
a heat-seeking missile, activated the targeting computer,
and pressed the fire button. There was a muffled whooshing
noise from below, and a bright dot arced out leaving a trail
of white smoke. It headed directly for one of the circling
hippies; and then, at the last moment, deflected up and out

over the East River. It exploded harmlessly in the sky, and a moment later they heard the concussion.

"As I thought," the Chief Programmer murmured.

"What the heck!" Sullivan was leaning forward in his seat belt. "Seemed like that fella just knocked the missile away! Like hitting a baseball with a bat! How about that!" He turned to Sullivan. "This a weapon test, or what? They got some kinda new defensive shield?"

"B.E.R.T.H.A. has regained its memory, I believe," said the Chief Programmer. He thumbed the comm switch. "Breen!"

"Yes, sir." The commissioner's face appeared on the screen.

"We have located the robot. It's in the Chrysler Building."

"Excellent, sir, I'll have my men—"

"It would eat your men for breakfast, commissioner. This is no longer a matter for the police. I will alert the nearest army and air-force bases. Meanwhile, I will personally need a secure underground command bunker, the deepest available. You will arrange that. I'm heading back to Roosevelt Island; you will provide me with an armed escort to Manhattan. Accompanying me is my personal assistant, and a passenger whose identity must be protected for security reasons. You will provide him with a combat suit and helmet, for purposes of disguise. Understood?"

He released the comm switch without waiting for Breen to reply.

22. VALUABLE OBJECTS

The commune members finished flight-testing their lifters late that afternoon. Burt mustered them in the Cloud Club, which had been remade as the building's command post since its botanical garden had been dismantled and redistributed to other floors.

"Okay, man, we got two hundred sky-pilots ready for whatever," Crosby reported.

Burt surveyed the hairy people standing or lounging around wearing bandanas, tinted granny glasses, ponchos, beads, belt-buckle peace symbols, earrings, bells, and other counterculture emblems of yesteryear. "Eight Miles High" was playing over the Muzak system, to boost morale. "But not everyone is present," Burt objected.

"Well, man, Lennon's cooling out in his bedroom, on account of the missile from that chopper totally freaked him."

"But it wasn't fired at him," said Melanie, standing beside Burt. "He wasn't even out there, was he?"

"Well, no," said Crosby, "but he saw it through the window. I mean, that is heavy shit, man. Him and a whole lot of other freaks got, uh, freaked, know what I mean?"

"Probably because they'd taken too many drugs," said Melanie. She turned to Burt. "You see?"

He patted her arm. "It is no sin to be afraid, Melanie."

"Hey, this is Woodstock Nation, man," Crosby complained. "We're not afraid of anything. It's just, if there's going to be helicopters and that, out there shooting rockets, and all we got to protect us is a little gadget made of bits of twisted wire—''

"I understand," said Burt. "All right, two hundred pilots will be sufficient." He raised his voice. "First I must reassure you, there is no reason to worry. When you are using a lifter, its field protects you from any weapon. You cannot even be affected by gas: the field will filter it. And because it taps the power that flows through the cosmos, it can never run down or wear out."

There were a few murmurs of "outasight" and "heavy" from the throng.

"Your mission," Burt continued, "is to bring back various important items. I have a list here. I will pin it to the wall. Each of you will choose an item, cross it off the list, and go out to find it."

There was an uneasy silence. No one moved.

Melanie tugged at Burt's sleeve. "Most of them have forgotten how to read," she whispered to him.

"Ah, I see. Well, here is a different plan. I will *tell* each of you which item to collect. We will begin now, starting here in the front row. First: Picasso's *Guernica* from the Museum of Modern Art. Next: a hard-core pornographic magazine. Its exact title is unimportant. Next: some assorted weeds. Next: a recent government talking newspaper. Next: a vinyl briefcase of the type carried by office workers in the midtown business district. Next—''

"Hey, hold it, hold it, man," said Crosby. "What is all this stuff?"

"Why, clearly, they are valuable objects," said Burt.

"You mean, we gotta go risk our necks for—"

"There is no risk, as I have just explained. You will simply take hold of what you want, and no one will be able to stop you."

"But that's *stealing!*" Melanie exclaimed. "Burt, how can you suggest such a thing!"

"I will explain that to you later," he said, beginning to sound somewhat defensive.

"We don't mind ripping off the capitalist pigs," a freak

in the front row spoke up. "We just want to know what you want this crap for."

Burt sighed. He stood in silence for a moment. "Because it is there," he said finally. "Look, I have given you the lifters. They are yours to keep. All I ask are these small favors in return. Please believe me when I say they are necessary to our future well-being. Indeed, our survival."

"All right, all right, man," said Crosby, waving the rest of the freaks silent. "A deal is a deal, even if it sounds crazy. Let's go on down the list."

"Thank you." Burt gave him a slightly strained benevolent smile. "Next: the head of the Statue of Liberty." He paused. "Six of you will be needed to fetch that, otherwise the lifters will not be sufficiently powerful. You will have to place it over the spire of this building, since it will be too large to bring inside. Also, I will have to give you a suitable saw. Next—"

He was interrupted by strange noises from the street.

"Burt! Quickly, come and look!" Melanie was peering out of the window.

Everyone came across the room and tried to see out. At one end of the 42nd Street bazaar, a pair of huge bulldozers had appeared. They began moving relentlessly down the street, plowing a swathe through the market stalls and peasant shacks. People were screaming and throwing rocks. Women and children were running in panic.

"I expected something of this sort," said Burt.

Beside him, a telephone rang. He had installed it and a video monitor an hour previously, linked with the communications terminal that Mick was constructing in the basement.

"Hey Burt?" Mick's voice came over the phone and his face appeared on the video screen. "I been patching into the city data network, like you showed me. I happened on some military cats making with guns and stuff. The army, you know? They're surrounding us, you dig?"

"This, too, I expected," said Burt. "They will probably attack the building tomorrow morning. But there is no cause for alarm. Their guns cannot harm us." He hung up the phone.

The hippies stared at him. There was an uneasy silence.

"Look, uh, no offense, man," said Crosby, "but it seems to me, I mean, the only reason they're hassling *us* is 'cause they want *you*."

"That is true," said Burt. "But they will assume I have shared some of my secrets. So, now, they will want you as well."

Another uneasy silence.

"Well, it was just a thought," said Crosby.

"Indeed. And now let me continue with my list of valuable objects. Next: a bicycle, preferably with tires. Next: a decorative painting on black velvet, such as are found in the homes of wealthier peasant people of Spanish descent." He paused. "Those of you who have been assigned objects to collect may leave now," he suggested. He waited till a few of the hippies started moving reluctantly toward the door. "All right. Next: a color portrait of Richard M. Nixon. . . ."

23. THE SEXIEST MAN ON THE PLANET

The bunker originally had been designed to sustain a garrison of men during nuclear bombardment. Under the Chief Programmer's orders, a team of laborers spent the previous afternoon ripping Spartan fixtures out of one wing and replacing them with deep-pile carpet, indirect lighting, a large bed, kitchen, ultrasonic shower, and state-of-the-art data-processing equipment. It was all ready in time for the Chief Programmer to spend the night there. Sullivan, meanwhile, was billeted in the unrenovated barracks next door. Citing reasons of national security, the Chief Programmer locked the ex-President in, muttering a few perfunctory apologies.

As morning dawned, the Chief Programmer lay on his back in bed while Charlotte, clad in a baby-doll nightdress and sucking a lollipop, lowered herself daintily upon him. "I do declare, you must be the sexiest man on the planet," she lisped, with a little sigh of simulated ecstasy.

"More," he told her. "Much more."

"Why, you just drive me crazy," she told him, polling her vocabulary of bedroom endearments. She squealed and bounced eagerly on his hard dark flesh. "You're so sexy, you make me wild! It feels so good it hurts! You're big and bad and powerful! You're tough! You're mean! You're nasty! Cruel! Hateful! Vindictive! Inhuman!"

His eyes glittered. "Yes!" he urged her on. "More!"

"You torture animals! You rape little children! You kill anything that breathes! You're a monster, a tyrant; a foul, despicable, brutal, demonic, poisonous, loathsome, warped, repugnant, twisted, stigmatiferous—"

"Ahhhhh!" he exclaimed, closing his eyes and clutching her synthetic flesh.

She relaxed on top of him, her plump artificial breasts pressing against his chest. "Was I good, hon?"

"The best, my sweet."

"That's 'cause I was programmed by the best." She giggled happily.

"Indeed you were." He yawned lazily and disengaged himself. "But it's time I attended to business."

"Oh, you." She pouted. "Always worrying about the world."

"Foolish of me, I know. But then, I was not so lucky as you. I had no one to program me. No cybernetic genius building a perfect balance of mind and body. I am a mere product of *God.*" He bared his teeth and scowled as he spoke.

"Oh, hon, I love you fine the way you are. Want some scrambled eggs with caviar and truffles on the side?"

The Chief Programmer belted his silver robe. "Why not?"

After breakfast she donned a skintight pink T-shirt and white shorts, and went around the huge room with a feather duster. The Chief Programmer reclined on the bed and watched her while he received his daily update from Computer Central. The room was completely dust-free, of course, but he always enjoyed seeing her tiptoe around on her high heels, reaching and stooping, humming to herself, faithfully serving him.

Reports flickered across the screen of his terminal. Gross national product, national debt, welfare rolls, famines, plagues, corporate bankruptcies, poison gas attacks, pogroms, military coups, massacres, hijackings, guerrilla insurgencies, and the usual rising birthrates. "Even in the face of our TV propaganda, they still persist in procreating," he mused. "But soon, soon it will all be different. With the implementation of macro-Darwinism—" He broke off as the internal phone chimed. "Yes?"

"A man, sir, here to see you. Says Commissioner Breen told him where to come." The face on the screen was that of a young National Guardsman whom the Chief Programmer had picked to act as his temporary personal lackey, mainly because of the man's total lack of imagination and initiative.

"Who is it?"

"Says his name is Henry Jackson. Also he has a woman with him—" There was a moment's offscreen consultation. "Says she's his wife."

"Send them both down here." He cut the connection. "Charlotte? The door." He pointed, and she obeyed, tottering on her high heels as she tugged at the heavy steel security portal.

Jackson arrived a few moments later, with his wife tagging along behind looking confused and distraught. "Come in, both of you," said the Chief Programmer. He studied Jackson's face. The features looked superficially the same, but had been completely remodeled in plastic.

He had a new head of artificial hair, his shoulders seemed broader, and his stoop was gone.

He turned his head slowly from side to side, as if scanning the room, then saw the Chief Programmer and gave him a glassy-eyed grin. He extended his hand with a whirring of motors. "Henry Jackson. Reporting for duty." There was a hollow, metallic ring to his voice.

"Very good." The Chief Programmer inspected Jackson with the critical eye of a connoisseur. "I see they got rid of that revolting old skin you were wearing last time I saw you."

"They got rid of it," Jackson echoed dumbly. He blinked, and his eyelids made a faint click-clicking noise. "They dumped it in the trash." He grinned again, and the plastic skin bunched realistically at the corners of his mouth.

"He came out of the hospital like this," Cynthia Jackson put in, unable to contain herself any longer. "I hardly recognized him. It's terrible! Henry said you promised there'd be no more mistakes at the hospital. You promised! And now look at him!"

"I can hardly see this as a mistake, Mrs. Jackson," the Chief Programmer said. "On the contrary, it's a considerable improvement. Last time I saw this man, he was a mental and physical wreck. Tell me, Jackson, are you happy now?"

"I am happy now," he echoed. He flexed his shoulders. "Reporting for duty. Henry Jackson."

"Good, good. And I suppose you're interested in that job I mentioned."

"I am interested in that job. You bet. Ready, willing, and able. Arrest, detain, assault. Kick ass." He paused momentarily, as if confused. "Reporting for duty," he added, and grinned some more.

"Well, I can see we still have to make a few adjustments, but nothing major. You can be my personal assistant. They replaced your whole brain, did they?"

"They replaced my whole brain, yes, correct. No problem. Piece of cake."

Mrs. Jackson slumped down on a chair. "After all our years together," she said blankly. "Can anything be done?"

"You mean, restore him to his old, wretched, neurotic, imperfect human form?" The Chief Programmer shook his head. "Impossible. And undesirable, too."

"But . . . there's no one left to look after me!"

"Hah," said Jackson. "That's tough." He laughed mechanically.

Mrs. Jackson pulled out her handkerchief and started sobbing. The Chief Programmer gave a little grunt of disgust. Naked emotion always offended his sensibilitics. "Charlotte, take her away. Or . . . on second thoughts, take her next door. Sullivan always complains I deprive him of female companionship." He glanced at Mrs. Jackson and smiled faintly to himself.

"No, I want to go home!" she moaned.

The Chief Programmer shook his head. "For the next few hours, the streets of New York may be somewhat, er, eventful. Charlotte?" He gestured.

"Upsy daisy!" Charlotte grabbed Mrs. Jackson's arm and hauled her to her feet. She quickly hustled the woman out of the room, ignoring her plaintive objections.

"Now, Jackson," said the Chief Programmer. He walked to the workbench he had had installed and opened a case of small, exotic tools. "Time for a little fine-tuning, my old friend. What do you say to that?"

"Time for a little fine-tuning." Jackson grinned and grinned.

The Chief Programmer seated Jackson on a chair, opened the inspection hatch at the back of his head, and calmly began work. "I hope they retained some of your old personality," he said. "Tell me, Jackson, your feelings toward the Negro race."

"Jungle bunnies," said Jackson. He sniggered. "Buncha dumb fucks."

"That's my boy." The Chief Programmer twisted an adjustment screw with a savage little flick of his wrist. Jackson jerked in the chair and let out a strange, fractured yelp.

Meanwhile, very faintly, from high above, the thump-thump of huge explosions began.

24. DEMOLITION

Down in the basement, Mick noticed a sudden high-pitched whistling noise, almost at the limit of human hearing. It seemed to be coming from the stacks of garbage cans. When he touched one of them, he discovered it was perceptibly warm.

He started up the emergency stairs. The building shook suddenly under his feet, and he heard muffled explosions from outside in the street. He climbed the stairs faster, feeling the windowless concrete walls of the stairwell closing in. The candle he carried to light his way flickered in sudden gusts of air, and the building trembled again around him. By the time he finally reached the Cloud Club, he felt the floor swaying from side to side.

He found Crosby at the door, even more dissipated and dragged-out than usual. His eyes were bloodshot and his face twitched intermittently. "What's shaking?" said Mick.

"This whole damned building is shaking, man," said Crosby. "You come to see Burt? He said he didn't want to be disturbed, but I guess you're okay."

"Yeah, I guess I am." Mick hurried into the room and shaded his eyes from the bright morning light. The place was cluttered with trophies and bric-a-brac that Burt's teams of flying hippies had brought during the previous afternoon. Mick skirted the piles of junk and found Lennon, Burt, and Melanie standing in a group at one of the windows overlooking the street.

Burt turned to greet him. "Mick, what brings you here?

Is anything wrong in the basement? Why did you not use the phone?''

"I had to get the hell out of there," said Mick. "The cans started making a kind of a whistling noise, and started heating up, and the building started shaking—" He broke off as there was a protracted rumbling from the street, and the floor swayed some more.

"Do not be alarmed," said Burt with a smile.

Mick joined Melanie and Lennon at the windows, just in time to see the skyscraper opposite collapse in huge clouds of dust and cascades of rubble. The smoke gradually cleared, revealing the street engulfed in gigantic mounds of masonry and twisted steel.

"Powerful explosives were placed around the base of our building during the night," Burt explained, "and were detonated a short while ago. However, we are now completely enclosed in a force field—a large version of the field created by the lifters. When a weapon is directed against it, it reflects the energy. With unfortunate results." He pointed to the remains of the building opposite.

Mick walked around the room and looked out of the other windows. On all sides, buildings had collapsed. The Chrysler Building was standing alone in a sea of rubble.

Mick made his way back to Burt. Moving around the Cloud Club was difficult: pieces of sculpture, home furnishings, gadgets, oil paintings, and other miscellaneous memorabilia were piled to the ceiling. "You get the head off the Statue of Liberty?"

"There was insufficient time, unfortunately," said Burt.

Lennon cleared his throat. He looked paler than usual, and his eyes moved nervously. "Think there'll be any more trouble?"

"Oh, yes. Next, they will drop bombs," Burt said. He had his arm around Melanie, who was saying nothing, staring blankly out at the devastation.

"Don't you think maybe we oughta keep our heads down; get back from the windows, and like that?" Mick suggested.

Burt shook his head. "The field will protect us."

"Yeah, but the vibration alone—"

"The monomolecular film has sealed the building. That will maintain the structural integrity.

"There!" said Melanie. She pointed.

Black silhouettes were flying in from the east, out of the sun.

Melanie gave a little cry and clutched at Burt. Mick instinctively backed away. There was an awful moment of anticipation in which nothing happened, and then the building shook with concussions as bombs exploded all around in sheets of blinding yellow-white light.

Mick picked himself up off the floor. He tried to blink away the afterimages swimming in his eyes. He saw Lennon lying flat on his back and crawled across to him. "You okay?"

"I think he fainted," said Burt.

Lennon groaned, and his eyelids flickered. "Om," he said faintly. "Om, om, om . . ."

"Guess he can handle it," said Mick. He glanced across at the exit, and saw Crosby had fled. "What about the rest of the commune? They must be shitting in their pants."

"I believe they resorted to a variety of drugs," said Burt. "I imagine many of them are unconscious."

"Uh-huh." Mick looked at Melanie, who was still clutching Burt and staring with wide eyes at nothing in particular. "You okay?" he asked her.

She nodded dumbly.

"So what is this secret stuff you know," Mick asked Burt, "that makes 'em blow up half Manhattan just to get at you?"

"They have demolished only a few city blocks," Burt corrected him, "in a part of town that was overdue for urban renewal."

"Well, all right, but that don't answer the question."

"No." Burt paused. "I am reluctant to answer you, Mick. It is in my programming not to interfere in human affairs unless I am forced to do so. With the exception of my acquiring these valuable objects"—he gestured at the heaps of memorabilia—"I have not imposed my will upon the people of this world in any way. I have merely taken steps to protect myself. And the theft of these pieces is justifiable in that I have provided the people of Earth with items of advanced technology infinitely more valuable than that which I have gathered here.''

Mick eyed the heaps of junk. A parking meter was standing beside him, next to a stack of cold hamburgers and a tandem pedmobile. ''Looks almost like my pad on the island.'' He thought about his home, and felt a pang of nostalgia. ''So what happens next?''

Burt shrugged. ''I do not know.''

''I linked our comm equipment with all the data circuits you asked for,'' Mick said, nodding toward the screen, phone, and keyboard on a table nearby. ''You can patch through to the guys out there calling the shots if you want.''

''Thank you, Mick.'' He made no move toward the equipment.

Mick shook his head. ''Don't like to seem as if I'm cutting out on you, dad, but it don't seem as how there's much left for me here.''

Burt looked at him inquiringly. Melanie blinked and slowly focused on him. ''Mick, you don't mean you're going away?''

''Thinking about it, babe. Told you this was just an overnight stay.''

''But Mick, it isn't safe outside!''

''Hell of a lot safer than in here,'' he said. ''Seems to me, just yesterday I was on my island. Even had me some company.'' He thought of Cynthia Jackson and wondered briefly if she might still be over there. ''Another thing: I drove my car into the ditch. Gotta pull it out.''

''Your car! Mick, this is no time to worry about your car!''

''Well, you got your worries, I got mine.''

''You would be welcome to stay with us,'' Burt said.

''With all these freaky guys?'' He glanced at Lennon still stretched out on his back. ''I got the old cats in Fun City to think about. They depend on me for food.''

Burt spread his hands. "If you wish to leave, I will provide you with a lifter. If you fly down among the buildings, you should evade detection. I will give you plans, also, for a power generator, so that you can enclose your home and protect it in the same way that I have protected us here." He paused. "It will shield you from all forms of weapons."

Another huge explosion boomed outside. A second wave of airplanes had come in, and bombs were exploding all around, although the noise was oddly muffled, filtered by the protective shield.

When he picked himself up off the floor again, Mick found Burt placidly sketching a diagram. "There. Take this, and this." He handed him a lifter. "It is best to leave now, while there is no danger."

"No danger. Sure."

"I can't believe you're going," said Melanie. "I'll miss you."

"You and me, babe, never was picked to click. But I'll miss you too." He gave her a quick hug. Then he turned to Lennon, still lying flat on his back. He leaned over the onetime guru. "Take it easy, dad."

Lennon opened his eyes. "You copping out?"

"You got it." Mick winked at him.

"I will unseal the roof exit," Burt said. He went to the door, ran a rewired pocket calculator around its edge, and pulled it open. "Be sure to erect the defensive field as soon as you get to the island," he told Mick. "That is extremely important."

"I hear you. So long, daddy-o." He grabbed Burt's hand, gripped it briefly, than strode out the door and up the stairs to the roof.

While Burt resealed the exit, Melanie ran to the window. "There he goes!" She watched Mick drift out and down, his body glowing with a faint green aura. "Oh no!" she cried. "They're shooting at him!"

Gun emplacements had opened fire with tracer bullets. Flak exploded around the black-jacketed figure.

"He will not be hurt," Burt assured her. And as he

spoke, Mick drifted out of the clouds of smoke. He paused a moment, made an OK sign with his finger and thumb, then turned and flew down among the buildings that were still standing at the edges of the zone of rubble. Within moments, he had disappeared among them.

25. NUKE THE KOOKS

The Chief Programmer had donned a black flannel suit, white shirt, and black leather shoes. He reclined comfortably in his chair. "All right, Jackson, you know what to do."

Henry Jackson kneeled at his feet, a can of boot polish in one hand and a cleaning rag in the other. "Sure 'nuff, boss. I put a shine on dese shoes you can see your face in. Yes, sir!"

"Very good, Jackson. Begin."

The ex-human, ex–police chief started working industriously. "I clean all your shoes, boss. I clean 'em so good, you ain't never seen dem shoes so clean before, yes *sir*, boss!"

The Chief Programmer set aside his set of cranial adjustment tools, congratulating himself on a job well done. "After you finish the shoes," he told Jackson, "you can scrub the toilet."

Jackson nodded enthusiastically. "I do anything you want, boss, you jus' ask Jackson, he do it for you, sho 'nuff!"

While Jackson started work on the second shoe, the Chief Programmer reached across to his communications console. He flipped a couple of switches, and several screens lit up, showing Sullivan's quarters next door from a variety of hidden cameras. The ex-President was pacing to and fro, thumbs tucked in the pockets of his waistcoat, while Cynthia Jackson sat watching him admiringly, with her hands clasped in her lap.

"The people," Sullivan was musing aloud. "What were their geographic and ethnic origins? Were they confined to a narrow socioeconomic stratum, or did we have a more broadly based constituency? What was their wealth index and consumer-choice profile? Yes, sir, it was a toughie."

"I never realized politics was so complicated," Cynthia Jackson simpered.

"Yep," said Sullivan. He nodded sagely.

"And that's how you became President?"

"Um-hm." He continued pacing.

"You know, you look different than on the TV. You look more distinguished."

"Thank you. Thank you kindly, m'dear."

"I don't remember your hair gray at the edges like that."

Watching on the closed-circuit monitor, the Chief Programmer made a mental note to add gray tones to the hair on Sullivan's robot look-alike in Washington, just in case.

"You know, you deserve better," Cynthia Jackson continued, looking with disapproval at the rows of bunks that had been built to accommodate National Guardsmen. "A man of your position shouldn't have to live like this, not ever. That was the trouble with my husband. He never stuck up for his rights. Never really took care of me properly, you know."

"Damn shame, fine figure of a woman like you." Sullivan walked across and sat down beside her. He slapped his hands on his knees. "Tell me, ah, your husband, is he—"

"He wouldn't listen to me," she said sadly. "All he cared about was his job." She sighed. "And now he's permanently disabled. I shall be suing for divorce. What else can I do?"

"Ah. Ahem." He patted her on the shoulder, and left his hand there, feeling her soft, plump flesh. "My sympathies."

The Chief Programmer switched off the monitor. He looked down at Jackson, who was just finishing the second shoe. "Hear that, boy? Your wife's given up on you."

"Wife?" Jackson stopped and spoke the word slowly, strangely. He looked around as if expecting to find her nearby.

"Forget it, you don't have a wife. Pack up your polish and go over there in the corner."

Faced with a direct order, Jackson clicked back into gear. "Yes sir, boss!" He grinned and nodded and backed away.

The Chief Programmer reseated himself at his communications console. Enough entertainment; time to return to work. He typed some codes to activate monitor systems in drone aircraft circling the Chrysler Building. The screens lit up, showing the building untouched amid total devastation.

The Chief Programmer eyed it vexedly. He punched a series of numbers. "Breen?" He had chosen to retain the commissioner as liaison with the special forces assaulting the building.

"Yes sir!" Breen's face appeared on another screen. "I've been trying to reach you, sir."

"I've been busy. Did they make the bombing runs?"

"Yes, sir. But the building seems to possess some kind of defense system that we don't understand. This may sound hard to believe, but it seems to resemble some sort of invisible protective shield."

"Indeed." The Chief Programmer drummed his fingers.

"We evacuated a large number of city residents overnight, but many others refused to move or were left behind," Breen went on. "There could be thousands trapped under the rubble." He shifted uneasily. His face was pale. "I hope you realize, even with our usual control over the media, the repercussions—"

"Of course I realize. None of this is your responsibility,

Breen. It was directed not only by the President, but by the World Council.'' He stared at the man steadily.

"But you're demolishing the city!'' Breen blurted out. "It's chaos out there! Eight blocks reduced to rubble, windows broken for miles around—people are rioting; the police have had to barricade their headquarters for their own safety; the peasants are trying to burn it down—what's *happening?*''

"I will attempt to negotiate with our fugitive,'' said the Chief Programmer. "In the meantime, I suggest you take shelter underground.'' He broke the comm link. "Charlotte! Go get Sullivan. Tell him . . . tell him that his hour has come.''

"Sure thing, hon! Be right back!'' She exited on high heels.

The Chief Programmer stared moodily again at the video image of the Chrysler Building gleaming in the hazy sunlight. It was hard to tell from the monitor screen, but the building seemed to be enveloped by some kind of weird green glow.

"All right, what's the story?'' said Sullivan, flopping into a chair opposite.

The Chief Programmer looked up. "Good morning, Sullivan,'' he said with mild distaste. "You have been enjoying the company of Mrs. Jackson?''

Sullivan gestured irritably, as if to dismiss the topic. He glanced around at the large room. "See you set yourself up in the lap of luxury, eh? Spared no expense.''

"The perquisites of power, Sullivan. No doubt you remember them.''

"Hm. Hm.'' He linked his fingers across his stomach and shot the Chief Programmer a wary glance. "So what's the meaning of that message your puppet just came and told me? What the heck has been going on in here, anyhow? And up there, for that matter.'' He jerked his thumb at the ceiling.

The Chief Programmer settled back in his chair. "Our attempts to destroy the runaway robot have been unsuccessful.''

"Aha! Got away from you, did it?"

"Not at all. So far as I know, it is still in the Chrysler Building. But it has erected some sort of screen that deflects all conventional weapons. As a result, it remains unharmed, while surrounding buildings have been reduced to rubble. Local residents who were stupid, obstinate, or unlucky enough to remain in the vicinity have been buried alive."

"Uh?" said Sullivan.

The Chief Programmer slapped his hands down on his desk. "It's a total fiasco, Sullivan. We've destroyed several city blocks and wiped out several thousand peasants. And we haven't even done the job efficiently."

"Hold your horses, now, just a minute here. I still don't understand what you want this robot for in the first place. You never did tell me. At least, I don't think you did, did you?"

The Chief Programmer sighed. "For your information, robot B.E.R.T.H.A. was online with Computer Central during its, ah, manufacture. It had free access to highly classified data. It was also designed to be many times more intelligent than a normal human being. I intended it to participate in implementing our global scenario. Now that it has escaped, violated its own programming, and recovered its memory, it is a menace to world peace and, indeed, to life as we know it."

"Is it, by golly. Well, now you're talking."

"I certainly am, Sullivan, which you may take as a measure of my desperation." He studied the ex-President shrewdly. "In view of your long history of public service, and your extensive experience of political affairs, I wonder if you have any advice to offer."

Sullivan's eyebrows moved up and down and his forehead furrowed in thought. He pulled at his chin, pulled at his earlobe, shrugged, and thrust his hands into his pockets. "Seems to me like you opened up a can of worms."

"Your insight is remarkable."

"Does this here robot speak English? Maybe you can negotiate with it."

The Chief Programmer gave a thin smile. "Excellent idea. In fact, I was hoping you might volunteer."

"Now, wait a gosh-darned minute. I mean to say—"

"It has to be you, Sullivan." He spoke with sudden decisiveness. "Having had free access to Computer Central, the robot must know that your look-alike in Washington is nothing more than an output device. You, on the other hand, are *irreplaceable*." He stared at Sullivan with what he hoped was wide-eyed sincerity. "I propose that you go to the Chrysler Building as a gesture of good faith. If necessary, you will remain there while the robot surrenders to us. Its safety will be a guarantee of yours, and vice versa. That seems a fair exchange."

"You want me to be held hostage?" Sullivan started up out of his chair.

"For the sake of world peace, Sullivan. You realize, there could be a Nobel Prize in this for you. And certainly"—he glanced around at the opulence of the room—"you will be rewarded with the privileges and comforts befitting a man who achieved such a triumph."

"But just a gosh-darned minute." He scratched his head vigorously.

"I will contact Breen and arrange ground transportation," said the Chief Programmer.

"That will not be necessary." The voice came from a loudspeaker in the communications console. It was polite, calm, and without any particular accent.

The Chief Programmer froze.

"I have been online for the past few minutes," the voice went on, "listening to your conversation. We tapped into your network earlier this morning, just before your attack began."

"It's the robot, by George!" Sullivan exclaimed.

The Chief Programmer started typing on another keyboard, attempting to trace back through the system. The display in front of him suddenly went dead. He stared at it, and his face twitched.

"I have no more use for Mr. Sullivan than you seem to," Burt's voice continued. Faintly, in the background, people were chanting something about "Give Peace a Chance." "All I wish is that you should leave me and my friends alone. If you continue to attack us, I will reveal everything I know, to all the people of the world."

There was a click, and the transmission cut off.

"Well, how do you like that." Sullivan stood up, leaned over the console, and rapped his knuckles on it. "You come on back. We're willing to talk turkey, you hear?"

The Chief Programmer waved Sullivan away. "Forget it." He studied the array of controls in front of him, but touched none of them.

There was a noise from the corner of the room. A shuffling footstep, and then another. "Robot?" said Henry Jackson.

Sullivan and the Chief Programmer both turned to look at him.

Jackson shuffled forward. "Apprehend suspect." His voice was a clumsy, halting monotone.

"Keep out of this, fella," said Sullivan. "You got a couple of screws loose, seems to me."

"His reprogramming was hastily done," said the Chief Programmer. "The voice of the robot must have triggered an unerased memory."

Jackson reached the communications console and stopped. His face widened in an idiot grin. "You wasting your time, boss."

"To hell with this nonsense," Sullivan complained.

The Chief Programmer ignored him. He studied Jackson. "If we're wasting our time, Jackson, what do you suggest?"

"Dope addicts. Weirdo faggots. Nuke 'em."

"That's the first sensible suggestion I've heard this morning. Thank you, Jackson."

Sullivan shook his head, making his jowls wobble. "Have you gone raving mad?"

"Jackson!" The Chief Programmer's voice was a peremptory command. "Rip the wire out of that extension phone."

Jackson twitched and seemed to wake up. "Yessir,

boss!'' He seized the wire in his prosthetic hands and tore it loose.

"Now use it to tie this fool to the chair over there."

"Get him away from me!" Sullivan shouted. "You goddamn lunatic, you want to kill us all?"

Jackson grabbed Sullivan by the neck and threw him into the chair with inhuman strength. "It'll just be a tactical warhead," the Chief Programmer remarked. "This bunker is bombproof. We'll be perfectly safe."

"No!" Sullivan yelled as Jackson started binding his wrists to the arms of the chair.

The Chief Programmer punched the code for a nearby air base. "I already have a plane standing by. It shouldn't take more than fifteen minutes to wrap this up."

26. WATCH THE BOMB

In the lull following the last attack, a number of commune members had made their way up to the Cloud Club. They sat amid the heaps of memorabilia, hands linked, holding a peace vigil under Lennon's guidance, chanting "No war! No war!" and "We Shall Not Be Moved" while Burt and Melanie stayed by the phone, listening in on events at the Chief Programmer's bunker.

"Nuclear weapons!" Melanie cried. "Did you hear that, Burt? He said they're going to use nuclear weapons on us!"

Her voice was loud enough to reach most of the hippies. The chanting stopped abruptly. Some people yelled a few rounds of "No nukes! No nukes!" out of long-standing habit, but this quickly died away into uneasy murmuring and apprehensive glances.

"Nothing to worry about," Burt told his audience. "I have already taken precautions."

Mistress Ursula stood up in the crowd. "That's what you scientists always say!" she cried. "You become intoxicated by power. You think you are infallible. You seek to force the pattern of things. *Remember Three Mile Island!*" She pointed a finger at him as if uttering a medieval curse.

Burt was unmoved. He turned to Melanie. "Come, my sweet, let us go out for a stroll on the balcony. We can watch them drop the bomb. It will be a unique experience."

"He's out of his mind!" Ursula wailed. "We must run, run away while there is still time!"

"The doors were sealed yesterday," Burt pointed out. "And in any case, they are now under thirty feet of rubble. You will have to trust me, Ursula."

"Everything he's said has worked out fine so far," said Lennon.

"But that's what scientists *always* say!"

"Come, Melanie." He took her arm. "We should not miss this."

"Burt, are you sure?"

"There is no risk." He unsealed the exit door and escorted her out while the hippies watched apprehensively.

On the observation deck the air smelled fresh and clean. The protective field had filtered out all impurities. It shimmered as a faint green curtain enveloping the building. "I believe this will soon be over," said Burt. "And then we can all relax."

"Relax!" Melanie shook her head. She thought suddenly of Mick. "What if Mick hasn't had time to protect himself on the island yet?"

"He too will be safe. You will see."

"I don't know, Burt. You said yourself, even a superhuman person makes mistakes once in a while." She chewed at her thumbnail. "Burt?"

He had been scanning the horizon for aircraft. "Yes, Melanie?"

"I'm really sorry I wouldn't talk to you yesterday morning."

"Don't worry about that. I understand."

"It's just that I used to watch a lot of movies, you know, and I started thinking you were this thing from another world, you know, like in *I Married a Monster from Outer Space?*"

"I have not seen that movie. In fact, I have not seen any movies."

"I guess you haven't. Well, I was wrong, Burt. You're a wonderful person." She stopped in embarrassment. "I just wanted to say that."

"Thank you, Melanie. I admire you, also. Look there!" He pointed to a faint contrail, high in the sky, heading directly toward the Chrysler Building.

"Oh Burt!" She clutched at him. "If I'm going to die—"

"You are not."

"But I might. And I just wanted to tell you one more thing."

"What is that?"

"I love you too, Burt." She buried her face quickly in his shoulder.

He stroked her head. "I am glad," he said. "There now, I think they must have released the bomb. See, the plane has turned. We must allow for the forward velocity, as well as the downward pull of gravity, shaping a parabola . . . Look, Melanie!"

"No, no, I don't want to see."

"But here it comes!"

Despite herself, she lifted her head. A tiny black dot was coming out of the sky, growing microscopically larger, without any other perceptible motion, in complete silence. Then suddenly it grew much bigger, frighteningly fast. Melanie gave a little cry of panic. She flinched. But at the last possible instant, there was a little ripple in the green curtain surrounding the building. The dot bounced away, directly upward. It vanished quickly into the dome of the sky.

There was a long, empty moment of silence. "You see?" he told her. "It did not even explode. By now, it has reached escape velocity. It will leave Earth forever."

"Oh." Melanie felt shaken. In a way, she realized, she was even a little disappointed.

"We must go inside," Burt said. "And, since our attackers have ignored my warning, I will do what I told them I would do."

"What's that?" she asked numbly.

"I will tell the people of the world everything that I know."

27. CORRUPT, INCOMPETENT, OR BOTH

The Chief Programmer brooded in his bunker, surrounded by banks of video monitors. He watched the nuclear warhead fall, watched it bounce harmlessly off the Chrysler Building, and watched it disappear into the blue. "So much for that," he said to himself.

"What happened?" Tied to his chair, Sullivan was unable to see.

"Same thing as when we were in the helicopter and I shot the missile at that flying freak." The Chief Programmer sat back in his chair, pondering deeply.

"Troubles, huh, hon?" said Charlotte, always quick to notice if her beloved mentor should become morose. "Shall I make you a little something? How about a banana daiquiri?"

"Later, perhaps, Charlotte."

"Wan' me go clean dat toilet, boss? Huh boss?"

"Not right now, Jackson, no."

"Tarnation, man, can't you shut these puppets up?" Sullivan struggled in his bonds.

"They're all I have, Sullivan, to preserve my sanity." He drummed his fingers. "I think perhaps—" He broke off suddenly. The picture of the Chrysler Building jumped and fragmented. In its place appeared a long shot of the White House in Washington. "What the hell?" He flipped to a different channel, and then another. The same picture was being transmitted on all of them.

The National Anthem started playing. Sullivan twitched, reflexively attempting to stand up.

The Chief Programmer switched to the government-run TV networks. They, too, showed the same transmission.

"And now, the President of the United States." There was a slow cross-fade to a man sitting behind a large wooden desk. With the exception of the hair above his ears, which had not yet turned gray, he looked exactly like R. Folsom Sullivan.

"What in heaven's name is going on?" Sullivan shouted.

"They patched through to your double in Washington somehow," the Chief Programmer said. "That means they're overriding Computer Central. Jesus Christ!" He started punching buttons.

"If a daiquiri won't do, how about a mai-tai, hon?"

"My fellow Americans," said the robot President.

The Chief Programmer's fingers flew across his keyboards, issuing access codes and priority commands. Lights winked festively. A loudspeaker burped, buzzed, then transmitted a scratchy recording: "We're sorry, your call cannot be completed as dialed. . . ."

The Chief Programmer slumped back in his chair. He stared numbly at the systems, then turned his attention back to the TV screen.

"Things have not been going very well lately," the robot President remarked. He paused, adopting a frown of grave concern.

The Chief Programmer reached again for his keyboards,

then let his arms fall onto the surface of the desk in front of him.

"Many people in the world are not very happy right now," the President went on. "Some of them don't have jobs anymore. In foreign countries, a lot of people are dying of starvation. Wars are killing people with unpleasant new weapons, and we are running out of oil. As if this isn't bad enough, the Antarctic ice cap is melting, so that towns in coastal areas will be submerged under fifty feet of water in the next few decades. I hate to have to say so, but that's how it is."

"Who in hell wrote this?" Sullivan complained.

"No one wrote it," said the Chief Programmer. "Someone's making it up as he goes along."

"You mean it's unscripted?" Sullivan sounded stunned.

"Now, with things in such a mess," the robot President continued, "you need to be able to count on your representatives in Washington. The trouble is, many senators and congressmen are corrupt, incompetent, or both."

"You've got to stop this," Sullivan entreated the Chief Programmer.

"There is nothing I can do," he said stonily.

"It's true," the President was saying. "Politicians spend so much time doing deals to get themselves reelected, they don't have time to keep track of what's really happening in the world, and they never look ahead more than four or five years. They're mainly interested in satisfying special-interest groups by spending public money on inefficient domestic programs that they can brag about to voters back at home. Meanwhile, the Centralized Global Computer Network—or Computer Central, as it is known—has taken over day-to-day economics, and even policy-making, worldwide. Maybe you remember when this system was set up, people demanded safeguards to stop it from falling under any one person's control. Well, here is the man who designed those safeguards."

The Chief Programmer's own face appeared suddenly on the screen. "Having designed the safeguards, he found it easy to get around them. He has become a secret dictator, with more power than the World Council. He controls Computer Central, and through it, he controls everyone else.''

"That true?'' Sullivan growled. "Eh? Is it?''

The Chief Programmer ignored him.

"This is not good news,'' said the robot President, shaking his head solemnly. "But there is worse to come. This dictator has imposed a plan on Computer Central which is designed to kill amost half the people in the world, beginning as early as next week. It involves poisoned relief supplies to underdeveloped countries, the release of mutant viruses from research laboratories, detonation of nuclear devices in selected areas, and more. This man believes the only answer to overpopulation is survival of the fittest. The World Council itself knows nothing about this. By the time they find out, it will be too late.''

"My God, that's just the kind of cockamamie craziness you would cook up if you had half a chance.'' Sullivan squirmed in his bonds. "Always said you couldn't be trusted.''

"Be quiet,'' the Chief Programmer told him tonelessly.

"This sounds awful,'' the President went on. "But it gets even worse. You see, three years ago, your President was secretly replaced by a look-alike. I am, in fact, that look-alike. The change was made so that Computer Central could present its plans and propaganda directly to the people, instead of through an unreliable, unpredictable human being. The presidential look-alike is not a human being at all. He is a robot.''

"Hah!'' Sullivan exclaimed. "Now it all comes out. Told you it would, didn't I? I always said people would wise up somehow, sooner or later.''

"Perhaps this seems a bit hard to believe,'' the President finished up. "You may not like the idea of your President being a robot. Well, I suppose I don't blame you. But I can prove it.'' He reached up and grasped his neck between his hands. There was a moment's pause, a clicking of latches, and then he lifted his head off and placed it on the desk beside him. "Good night, fellow

Americans," the head said. "At least, now, you know how things really stand."

The screen faded to black, then dissolved into static. There was a long silence. "Well, well," said Sullivan. "You know, seems to me they'll be needing me back in Washington before too long, once this sinks in. Maybe you better get me untied, hm? Maybe you'd better start remembering to call me Mr. President again. Eh? How's that grab you?"

"I said, shut up." The Chief Programmer flipped switches across the control panel, shutting down all external systems.

"Now, you listen here," Sullivan began. "I'm willing to grant you a Presidential pardon, but you gotta play ball, understand?"

The Chief Programmer stood up. "You're a fool. You think there's going to be anything left for you to govern? Computer Central is the only thing that's held the world together. Just suppose that broadcast went out worldwide, over every comsat, across every border. Can you imagine the results?"

Sullivan was silent for a moment. "Well, hey, there'll be some hollering, but we'll soon smooth things over—"

"Business as usual?" The Chief Programmer shook his head. "Not this time. But I'm wasting my breath. Charlotte! Jackson! Come." He strode toward the door, beckoning his mistress and his new aide to follow.

"Hey!" Sullivan shouted. "Come back here!"

The Chief Programmer found Mrs. Jackson loitering outside, where she had evidently been eavesdropping. She started back from him in alarm when she saw the look of cold anger on his face. "Get in there with Sullivan," he snapped at her. "Untie him, and he'll probably give you a Cabinet position." He turned to Henry Jackson. "What are you staring at? You don't know this woman. Get in the elevator."

"What? Yessir, boss, sorry, boss!"

"You too, Charlotte."

"Why sure, hon. We going back home to Colorado?" She batted her eyelashes at him.

The Chief Programmer joined them in the small steel car as its doors slid shut. "I think not," he murmured.

A little later, accompanied by Jackson and Charlotte, he headed south in a plane commandeered from the National Guard. For the time being, it seemed, some of his computer access codes still pulled their weight. He didn't like to speculate on how long that might last.

"But where are we going, hon?" Charlotte peered out through the Plexiglas in perplexity.

"Florida," he told her.

"Gee, that's nice! We can all soak up some sunshine!"

He shook his head. "Sorry to disappoint you, but it's going to be a short stopover."

"Oh, rats!" she pouted.

"I made arrangements, some years ago, in case of emergency. My private space vehicle is waiting in a silo at Cape Canaveral. We will ride it to low Earth orbit, refuel from a conveniently placed military satellite, then continue outward to the planet Mars."

"Mars!" she exclaimed. "Wow, I've never been there before!"

"Nor has anyone else," the Chief Programmer pointed out. "But Earth is beginning to irritate me. It'll be a long trip; still, with good company—" He glanced at his two companions. "The time should pass quickly enough."

28. BAD PROGRAMMING

"Man, you really have your shit together!" Lennon pounded Burt on the back amid a chorus of "Up the revolution," "Right on, brother," and "Power to the people!" from hippies in the Cloud Club. "Your revolutionary consciousness," said Lennon, "is right outa sight! You are where it's at!"

"A series of simple coded commands to the central computer enabled me to gain control of the Presidential robot," Burt told him, "so that I could dictate his speech."

Lennon nodded agreement, though he hadn't heard a word. "They'll be taking it to the streets now, brother. They'll sock it to the capitalist pigs of the world." He peered at the video monitor screen as if expecting the usual commentary from a panel of political analysts. But the government-sponsored network appeared to have shut down temporarily. A test pattern was being displayed, without any sound.

"I hope it does not provoke too much conflict," said Burt. "I tried not to make it inflammatory."

"You know, Burt, sometimes I think you don't understand people very well," Melanie told him.

He turned to her, ignoring the happy hippies clustered around. "What was that, Melanie?"

"You can't just go on television and tell everyone the truth! It'll cause more trouble than you can possibly imagine."

Burt looked puzzled. "Is it not correct to tell the truth?"

"Don't pay any attention to her," said Lennon.

"But she understands human nature better than I do. Melanie, what do you think will happen?"

"Gosh, I don't know! Now you've revealed this terrible plan to kill people—don't you think it may start a war or something?"

"But I had to tell innocent citizens what to expect. I was programmed, you know, to believe that truth and nonviolence are ideals to strive for."

He was interrupted by the video monitor. The test pattern had gone. A "Special Bulletin" title was being displayed above a picture of a rotating globe. There was an electronic fanfare, and a series of little beeps.

"This is gonna be good," said Lennon. "Sit down, sit down, let's see 'em talk their way out of this one."

The newscaster came on the screen. "A big hi and a how-are-you from Buddy Bentley, here in Washington, with the news you can trust." He grinned into the camera.

Burt studied the image on the screen, and frowned. He reached for the keyboard that he had used previously to control Computer Central.

"Burt!" There was a warning edge to Melanie's voice.

"Chaos and confusion, this A.M., were caused by a bizarre prank whose full extent is still not known." The newscaster was giving the cameras his best friendly grin. "TV screens all across America, and apparently in some foreign countries also, were taken over just minutes ago by a transmission which claimed to come from the White House in Washington. An actor, impersonating the President of the United States, made bizarre allegations about the World Council's upcoming peace plans and the integrity of legislators here in the capital." He grinned some more. "We don't yet know who the pranksters were who staged this one, but the FBI says it has already received information which—" He paused in mid-sentence.

Burt's fingers tapped busily on his keyboard.

"But that, of course, is just so much bullshit," the newscaster continued cheerfully. "The truth is, the broadcast aired earlier over these government-owned stations did come from the Oval Office. There are covert plans to wipe out a good proportion of the Third World. The President is a robot. And as for me, Buddy Bentley, I guess I have to tell you I'm a robot too." He took off his jacket as he spoke, then ripped his shirt open. "See, to save money, the network didn't bother to give me plastic flesh except where it would normally show. The rest of me is made of aluminum." He banged his metal arm against his metal chest. "And guess what? I don't have any legs. So that's what's happening in the world this A.M., and we'll have the regular news and weather for you at six. Be with us then."

"Groovy, baby!" the hippies shouted. "Far out, man!"

"Burt!" Melanie scolded him. "Haven't you caused enough trouble?"

"I—I'm sorry, Melanie." He looked at the keyboard under his fingers, as once again the commune members clustered around, congratulating him. "But it became evident to me the newsreader was not a real person, and I feared its lies would undo everything that I had tried to accomplish." He looked up at her hopefully. "I'm sure it is for the best. You know, my programming—"

"Maybe it was *bad* programming. And maybe you should try to think for yourself for a change." She turned away from him.

Meanwhile, some of the hippies had started singing. It was an old Bob Dylan song that some of them remembered from as far back as the Cuban Missile Crisis in 1962. The refrain kept returning to something about "A hard rain's gonna fall."

Afternoon faded into evening, and the air of Manhattan grew rank with smoke from hundreds of burning buildings. Mobs shouted in the distance, and there was the intermittent crackling of rifle fire. Squadrons of jet fighters flew overheard, helicopters were moving in the distance over Brooklyn, and the concussion of large field guns began echoing among those buildings that were still standing.

Inside the Cloud Club, the hippies continued celebrating

the downfall of the capitalist system, clustering around the TV set and jeering each new attempt by the government-sponsored network to reassure citizens that there was absolutely nothing to worry about. Buddy Bentley seemed to have been retired permanently; instead, a succession of politicians appeared, with awkward, fixed smiles and speeches that became more desperate and less convincing as the day wore on.

Finally, at six, there was another Presidential address. This time, the real R. Folsom Sullivan appeared before the cameras, accompanied by a group of the most trusted public figures in America—a famous football quarterback, several movie personalities, a tennis champion, and the 15-year-old star of the nation's longest-running TV situation comedy.

"Fellow Americans," said Sullivan.

The hippies groaned and blew raspberries.

"It's about time, by gosh, that someone gave you the scoop, straight from the shoulder." He nodded vigorously, as if he had just heard what he said, and agreed with it. "Now, I'm not going to try and tell you everything's hunky-dory. There hasn't been much plain dealing here in Washington. A couple years ago, I myself was pushed aside by the forces of progress. For a period of time, the untarnished truth is that this nation was being governed by a cellarful of radio parts. Well, you can bet your bottom dollar, we've taken steps to assure that this terrible condition will never be permitted to revert." The camera panned to a corner of the Oval Office, where the onetime robot President lay in a heap of smashed plastic pieces. "As of now, we have an honest-to-God human being back in charge," Sullivan went on. "Right, Joe?" He turned to the football player beside him.

"You bet, Mr. President!" He spoke in a carefully rehearsed monotone that viewers had grown to know and love in thousands of commercials endorsing chewing gum and automobile mufflers. He gave Sullivan a friendly punch in the shoulder, and turned to the camera. "This guy is sure enough the real thing!" He grinned fixedly.

"Thanks, Joe." Sullivan rubbed his shoulder. "That was quite a punch! Anyhow, fellow Americans, it's time to get this nation back on the straight and narrow track." The camera moved in slowly for a closeup. "Those who conspired under the democratic system will be incarcerated via the law of the land. Justice will be done, I will ensure that. In the meantime, let's all pull together. There's much to accomplish, but, together, we can accomplish—ah— much. Just ask what you can do for your country, and you'll soon see what your country can do for you." He hesitated, peering at his cue cards. "Your elected reprehensatives are back with a firm hand on the helm, we're hoisting new sails here at the Ship of State, bailing out the bilges, swabbing down the scuppers, and charting a new course toward peace and prosperity in the Land of the Free. God bless America, good night and, ah, thank you very much."

Melanie spent the night hugging her stuffed toy poodle, saying her prayers, and hoping for the best. She tried to get to sleep by reading some *True Romances* and humming lullabies to herself, but somehow she still felt anxious: somehow, somewhere, something was wrong.

Finally, as dawn light began creeping through the smoke that still suffused the outside air, she walked through the quiet corridors of the commune, and climbed the stairs to the Cloud Club.

She found him still sitting in front of the video monitor with the keyboard across his knees. The big room, cluttered with artifacts and mementos, seemed strangely forlorn. All the hippies had returned to their rooms overnight, leaving Burt alone.

"Hi," she said softly, padding across to him on bare feet. "What you been doing?"

He put the keyboard aside, looked up at her, and smiled sadly. "I have been trying to make everything work out right, Melanie. But they have disabled Computer Central now. No one seems to trust computers anymore. So there is little I can do, from here."

She sat beside him, sharing his chair. His physical presence was reassuring, even though it did seem as though he'd caused some trouble just lately, one way and another. He had good intentions, she told herself. Of course, there was the old saying about "the road to hell," but she didn't really believe that. Burt was a mental giant, a super-genius. He'd come up with something.

"The Soviet Union has invaded West Germany," he told her.

"They have?" Her cute features became clouded with concern. "How come?"

"It is hard to tell. American television is not broadcasting news anymore. It is showing old cowboy movies, and animated cartoons in which cats chase talking mice. My information comes from European stations, relayed by communications satellites. They say the whole of Europe will soon fall to the Soviet aggressors. Meanwhile, a nuclear weapon has exploded in Boston. In retaliation, the United States has bombed Tehran, although that may be a mistake, since Argentina is now claiming responsibility. In Africa—"

"Honey, stop, you're giving me a headache."

"We will all have big headaches before long, I think." He paused thoughtfully. "Perhaps it is time for us to go away somewhere, Melanie. The building's protective field will deflect missiles and protect against radiation; nevertheless, I doubt we would enjoy living here in the midst of surrounding nuclear devastation."

"I guess not." She couldn't think of anything else to say.

"I will make arrangements, to save ourselves and our friends."

"You mean the hippies have to come too? Oh, Burt, please!"

"I am responsible for their welfare. You have lived here all your life, Melanie. Surely you can tolerate their company for a few more days."

She pouted at him and hugged her arms across her frilly

pink nightdress. "Well, I guess I can, but what happens when we get where we're going?"

"There will be a wide variety of new friends to choose from."

"That sounds nice. Where do you have in mind?"

"Trust me, Melanie." He kissed her on the forehead, then stood up and walked to the middle of the room.

There was a long moment of silence. Melanie fidgeted in her chair. "Burt?"

He didn't answer. He stood with his eyes closed and his hands by his sides. His face had gone totally blank.

"Hey, Burt, what are you doing?"

"I am synchronizing my mind with the field generator in the basement." He let out his breath slowly. "There."

"Explain it to me in English, huh?"

He didn't answer.

Melanie gave him a vexed look. "You don't have to be so darned *mysterious* about it." She pushed back her chair and started to stand up.

The floor lurched under her. She sat back down with a little cry. "Burt, what's happening!"

There was a deep, growling, rumbling sound from far below. The floor started to vibrate.

"Is it an earthquake? Have they started dropping bombs again?" She clutched the sides of her chair.

The floor tilted. There was a scraping, grinding noise from beneath the building, and the thud-thud of falling chunks of rubble. Slowly, the Chrysler Building rose into the smoky air.

"Lift-off," said Burt with a serene smile.

"Oh wow!" Melanie managed to make it to the window. Outside, she saw the skyscrapers of New York City receding from view. The Chrysler Building continued moving smoothly upward, the floor now vibrating gently under her feet. The edges of Manhattan came into view. Dawn sunlight gleamed on the river and the sea beyond.

"I hope the people of the commune don't mind," said Burt. "I do think it is for the best."

She watched as the building rose still higher, revealing

most of Long Island and, to the west, New Jersey. Suddenly, there was a bright flash of light from directly beneath. "Burt!" Melanie cried. "Look there!" A mushroom cloud was already forming over Manhattan.

Burt nodded to himself. "I was afraid of that. We took off just in time."

29. LUST IN SPACE

"Jackson, I have told you before, *you do not have a wife.*"

The ex–police chief sat hunched in one corner of the spacecraft's cabin, holding his head between his hands as if he feared for the safety of his skull. "Yessir boss," he muttered thickly. He was silent for a minute. "Unfair," he added.

"Of course it's unfair!" The Chief Programmer was losing patience. "Whatever did you expect?"

Jackson scowled. "Beat their brains out. Downtown. Up the river. Kick ass."

"Get a grip on yourself," the Chief Programmer warned him.

"Anything you need, hon?" Charlotte floated in with a seductive smile. She smoothed her manicured hands across her tight red sweater, making her breasts bounce slowly in the zero gravity.

"Not right now," the Chief Programmer told her.

Jackson seemed to notice her for the first time. He chuckled stupidly. "Eat it or beat it, bitch."

"How dare you!" The Chief Programmer seized a cattle

prod that he had brought along in case of such an eventuality. "Jackson, it seems your reprogramming on Earth was incomplete. But cruder methods of behavioral training are still available. Let's see how many pain receptors they left you while you were in Bellevue." He jabbed Jackson with the tip of the prod, and there was a brief electric crackling sound.

"Ow!" Jackson cringed in his corner.

"Apologize to Charlotte. Say you're sorry for what you said."

Jackson's face went through a series of contortions. Finally, he mustered his sick, glassy grin. "Sorry, Miz Charlotte. Didn't mean nothing by it."

"On your knees in front of her." The Chief Programmer prodded him again.

Jackson yelped. In zero gravity, it was hard to get down on the floor and stay there, but he finally managed it, more or less. His knees floated an inch above the titanium plating.

"Repeat after me," said the Chief Programmer. " 'I will never speak that way to Charlotte again.' "

"Never speak dat way no more!"

"Well, that's better." The Chief Programmer looked from Jackson's prostrate form to Charlotte's tightly clothed nubile figure, and back again. "But we have to be absolutely certain, don't we, that those old memories aren't going to bother you again." He drifted backward and settled himself in his acceleration couch. "Crawl over here and lick my boots, boy."

"Yessir, boss!"

"And meanwhile, Charlotte, why don't you undress for me? Start with the sweater. Not too fast, now." He rested one foot comfortably on Jackson's neck, and pushed the other foot into his face. "Get busy, you!" he snapped, and jabbed him with the cattle prod again.

"Dat hurt, boss! You hurt Jackson!"

"It'll hurt a lot more if you don't learn to speak when you're spoken to." The Chief Programmer imagined all the pleasures lying in store during the next couple of years en route to Mars. The methodical and often painful reeducation of Henry Jackson could take at least that long.

Meanwhile, blushing and biting her lip, Charlotte was slowly working her sweater up over her swollen artificial flesh. She rotated her hips and jiggled enticingly, peeking out at the Chief Programmer from behind her blond curls.

He prodded Jackson once more for good measure and then relaxed, fingering himself idly. For the first time in his life, he realized, he had found pure contentment.

At that moment, an alarm sounded.

He was tempted to ignore it. But in a space vehicle, that wasn't wise. He grunted with irritation. "Neither of you move," he said, zipping his astro-overalls. "Just stay right there."

Jackson and Charlotte obediently watched their commander turn to his instruments.

The Chief Programmer stared at the screen in puzzlement. How could there be a proximity warning? He was fifty thousand kilometers from Earth, and nowhere near the Moon or the asteroid belt. He swung the scanner until something came into view. It was a tapering cylinder rotating slowly, coming in fast. It looked oddly familiar.

The Chief Programmer hastily calculated its trajectory. He reached for the attitude-control thrusters—and realized with dismay that they would do too little, too late. Suddenly, as the metal cylinder grew larger and filled the screen, he recognized it. It was the tactical nuclear device that had bounced off the top of the Chrysler Building and disappeared into the sky.

He barely had time to curse fate before the device impacted and exploded in a silent sheet of flame, instantly vaporizing his space vehicle, his companions, and himself.

30. FAR OUT

Lennon appeared in the doorway to the Cloud Club. His eyes were rheumy, and clumps of his white hair were sticking out at odd angles. He reached inside his robe to scratch his stomach, and yawned loudly. "Planes been bombing us again? Thought I felt the building shake." He shuffled across the room.

"Um, Daddy, prepare yourself for a surprise," said Melanie.

Lennon raised his eyebrows. "What's that?" Then he noticed something odd about the light, and glanced at the nearest window. Outside he saw brown landmasses and blue oceans drifting past. Planet Earth was a huge sphere rotating slowly against a backdrop of black, empty space. He stopped and stared at it for a moment. "Far out," he said. He stared at it some more. "What are those gray dots?"

"Mushroom clouds," said Burt. "While you were asleep, I'm afraid things went rather badly. The planet is now consumed in thermonuclear war, which I must admit is to some extent my fault."

"Well," said Lennon. He stared at the view for a while longer. "Well, it was bound to happen sooner or later, I guess."

"I took the liberty of bringing us up here," Burt went on.

"That's cool." Lennon nodded to himself. "I suppose it's lucky you did. But what are we going to breathe?

189

There isn't any air in space, is there? Seem to remember, I read that once.''

"I sealed the building," Burt reminded him. "And plant life has grown in such profusion on every floor, we will have ample oxygen. Also, you will find that many of the new plant species are edible."

"Macrobiotic," Lennon said approvingly.

Melanie clutched Burt's hand tightly. She was relieved that her father was taking things so well. "Do you want to know where we're going, Daddy?"

"Hm?" He blinked.

"I'm afraid Earth will not be hospitable to human life for a while," said Burt. "It may take a couple of years. Possibly a few centuries."

"That's a drag," said Lennon.

"Part of my programming—which, you will recall, I received originally from another star—instructed me to obtain items representing everyday life on your planet and send them back for exhibition in an interstellar museum." Burt gestured to the heaps of bric-a-brac and art objects scattered across the room. "In addition, I was required to include some specimens of the dominant Terran species, if at all possible."

Lennon scratched his head. "Let's get this straight. You want to take all this crap, and us with it, to some other part of the galaxy?"

"If that's all right with you. There's still time to drop you off, back on Earth, if you prefer. We can give you a force-field generator, such as the one I gave to Mick, and you'll be quite safe."

"You could help rebuild civilization, Daddy," Melanie told him. "It would be your chance to establish a new society better than the old."

Lennon muttered his mantra and meditated for a couple of minutes. "Screw it," he said. "I'd rather go someplace new. What'll they do, put us in some sort of zoo?"

"My instruction set is not entirely clear on that point," said Burt. "It will probably be an artificial planetoid to which representatives of other oxygen-breathing bipedal species have already been imported.''

''Honestly, Burt!'' Melanie scolded him. ''You simply *have* to learn how to speak so that other people can understand you.''

''I'm sorry.'' He looked chagrined. ''I mean, there will be other people, from races similar to yours, who've already gone through the same sort of experience. It will be like a zoo but much bigger, and we will be able to do what we like.''

''We?'' Lennon eyed him shrewdly. ''You're in on this?''

''I am indistinguishable from a human being,'' said Burt. ''Of course I must stay with you.''

Lennon stroked his beard. ''I better wake up the others. They'll want to talk this over, and they'll want to look at the view. It's trippier than a Fillmore West light show. I'll be right back.'' He headed for the exit.

''Burt?'' Melanie whispered. She tugged at his arm. ''Aren't you going to ask him?''

''What, you mean now?'' When he looked at her, he seemed to lose some of his serene confidence. His voice, too, lost its air of certainty, as though he no longer trusted his judgment.

''Yes, now!'' she insisted. She gave him a sharp nudge in the ribs. ''Go on!''

Burt took a deep breath. ''There is one more thing,'' he called out.

Lennon paused in the doorway. ''What's that?''

''I wish to marry your daughter.''

Lennon frowned. He took a couple of steps back into the room. ''You want to do *what?*''

''Don't be difficult about it, Daddy,'' Melanie warned him.

Lennon put his fat hands on his fat hips. ''There hasn't been a marriage in this commune since the day I founded it. This is the counterculture, not some plastic piece of Amerika. So long as I'm guru, *free love* is where it's at.

Sharing and caring. You don't own anyone else's body. Right?''

"You expect us to live in sin like you!" Melanie's voice rose quickly to a shrill pitch. Her cheeks turned pink. She clenched her fists. "I won't. As long as I live—"

"Just a moment." Burt patted her shoulder. "I will mediate, Melanie." He turned to Lennon. "You told me, I believe, that you surrendered your role as guru to me. And," he continued before Lennon could interrupt, "you said your daughter should be free to do her own thing."

Lennon opened his mouth and closed it a few times. He turned away. He turned back. He waved his finger at Burt. "Did she put you up to this?"

"We decided on it together," said Burt. "Just a few minutes ago."

Lennon groaned. "Jesus Christ, I'll never live this down."

Melanie let go of Burt and ran across the room. "Thanks, Daddy!" she exclaimed. She managed to overcome her natural revulsion toward his physical condition long enough to kiss him on the cheek.

He fended her off. "Just don't expect me to perform the ceremony," he warned her. "In fact, don't even expect me to attend it."

"I think perhaps Mistress Ursula may perform it for us," said Burt. "If we make her the honorary captain of this spaceship, she would be suitably qualified."

"And don't expect any wedding presents," said Lennon. "And when you want to get divorced, don't expect any help from me then, either." He brooded a moment, as if trying to think of anything else to disavow. "You are copping out," he finished up. "Selling out everything I stand for." He brooded some more. "You sure you want to go through with this?" he added finally, in a lower voice. "You, like, love this dude?"

"Of course. There isn't anyone else in the world I could ever love as much." Her eyes shone and her face became radiant.

Lennon glanced out of the window at the face of the

planet. "Seems to me there isn't anyone else in the world . . . period," he pointed out. "Still, I ought to be glad you found him when you did. He can keep you out of my hair." He sighed. "I better go tell Crosby. It's his fault, really. If he hadn't gone out and brought you back, none of this would have happened."

"Be careful as you descend the stairs," Burt warned him. "We are approaching orbital injection prior to our departure into interstellar space. There will be a period of weightlessness."

Lennon slapped his ample stomach. "Well, that's something to look forward to," he said as he walked out.

Melanie turned to Burt. "Oh, I'm so happy. Are you happy? I'm really happy. You make me so happy, I can hardly stand it."

"Do you love me," he asked, "even though I am less than human?"

"Burt, how can you even think such a thing! I love you exactly the way you are."

He hugged her to him, and they kissed.

EPILOGUE

In the Lunar Defense Installation, Eddie studied the video screen. It looked as if he was going to win his eighty-seventh straight game in a row. He did a quick mental calculation, then entered figures rapidly on the keyboard and watched intently for the result.

The screen suddenly went dead in front of him.

He blinked stupidly. "Hey, what's the problem?"

For a moment, there was no reply.

Eddie rubbed his eyes. He looked around at the room, focusing with difficulty on the familiar grimy furnishings. "I said, what's the problem?"

"I have received orders for you." Over the past six months, the computer had degenerated noticeably. Its voice had acquired an irritating lisp, and it tended to forget little things that Eddie told it.

"Can't this wait till tomorrow?" he complained.

"The United States is under attack. You must launch all missiles. I have armed and targeted the warheads."

"Is this a simulation?" Once in a while they pulled this kind of thing on him, just to make sure he was still awake.

"It is not a simulation."

Well, it didn't really make much difference. He had to follow the same routine either way. He went to the control panel, paged through the manual, and checked his codes. He punched them in on the keyboard, and added his password. "Okay? You got that?"

"Yes."

Suddenly the whole installation started vibrating. There was a muted roar as rockets blasted off nearby, carrying their cargos of death up and away. How about that, Eddie thought to himself. Those idiots back home really went and did it.

He sat back in his chair. "Come on, show me what's happening."

"You want to see broadcasts of events on Earth?"

Eddie rolled his eyes. "No, damn it. I want to finish the *game*." He waited impatiently until the flickering symbols reappeared on the screen. Then, with a distant, distracted smile, he continued to play.

About the Author

Robert Clarke, a slot-machine coin-evaluation system designer from Des Moines, Iowa, wrote science fiction in his spare time for twelve years with a pitiful lack of success. The manuscript of his first book, *Childhood's Troopers,* was lost in the mail when he submitted it to a publisher in 1963. His second work, *The Time Merchants,* disappeared when Lancer Books went bankrupt shortly after purchasing it in 1972. Undaunted, Clarke embarked on his magnum opus, the *Lord of Damnation* trilogy. Unfortunately, he modeled his protagonist on his brother— who, upon reading the manuscript, burned it.

Weary and embittered, Clarke wrote *Less than Human* in 1975, immediately before his untimely death in a choking episode at a fried chicken restaurant. Mindful of previous disasters, Clarke made no fewer than fifty photocopies of the manuscript before his demise. Many of these copies survived and were circulated among dedicated fans during the ensuing years. Ironically, this unofficial distribution of the book voided its protection under the copyright laws of its time, so commercial publishers refused even to consider it.

By 1984 most of the Xeroxes were seriously deteriorating. Clarke's son, Chuck, took on the task of reassembling and updating the novel as he believed his father would have wished. It is this completely rewritten version, copyrighted 1986 under Chuck's name, that you now hold in your hands.

Possibly, manuscripts of Clarke's early works still exist somewhere. In the meantime, *Less than Human* remains his only work ever to see publication.